"Our enemies outnumber us, but we are the superior force."

The Executioner rose to his feet. "Nenad's men are terrorists, not soldiers. They get others to commit their atrocities for them. But here in the jungle they are going to have to do their own fighting. They are not ready for what Niner Squad has become."

Cadet Jovich rose and the rest of the squad rose with him. "No way in hell they're ready for us."

"Caesar's men are jungle fighters, but they have been terrorizing unarmed villages for far too long. They are not ready for what you have become."

Cadet Eischen intoned Bolan's earlier words. "We shoot them until they're all down or we are."

Bolan shoved his right hand out into the middle of the circle. The rest of the squad huddled up and put their hands on top of his. "And though we walk through the valley of the shadow of death, we shall fear no evil...for we are Niner Squad, the apex predators and the meanest sons of bitches in the valley."

"Amen, Sergeant," Cadet Johnson said.

"On me, call out!" Bolan looked around and saw the steel in the backbone of his people. "Niner!"

The squad instantly shouted back, "Squad!"

Bolan raised his hand beneath the squad's and they snapped their hands down to break the huddle. "Be ready to move in an hour."

MACK BOLAN®
The Executioner

#319 Entry Point
#320 Exit Code
#321 Suicide Highway
#322 Time Bomb
#323 Soft Target
#324 Terminal Zone
#325 Edge of Hell
#326 Blood Tide
#327 Serpent's Lair
#328 Triangle of Terror
#329 Hostile Crossing
#330 Dual Action
#331 Assault Force
#332 Slaughter House
#333 Aftershock
#334 Jungle Justice
#335 Blood Vector
#336 Homeland Terror
#337 Tropic Blast
#338 Nuclear Reaction
#339 Deadly Contact
#340 Splinter Cell
#341 Rebel Force
#342 Double Play
#343 Border War
#344 Primal Law
#345 Orange Alert
#346 Vigilante Run
#347 Dragon's Den
#348 Carnage Code
#349 Firestorm
#350 Volatile Agent
#351 Hell Night
#352 Killing Trade
#353 Black Death Reprise
#354 Ambush Force
#355 Outback Assault
#356 Defense Breach
#357 Extreme Justice
#358 Blood Toll
#359 Desperate Passage
#360 Mission to Burma
#361 Final Resort
#362 Patriot Acts
#363 Face of Terror
#364 Hostile Odds
#365 Collision Course
#366 Pele's Fire
#367 Loose Cannon
#368 Crisis Nation
#369 Dangerous Tides
#370 Dark Alliance
#371 Fire Zone
#372 Lethal Compound
#373 Code of Honor
#374 System Corruption
#375 Salvador Strike
#376 Frontier Fury
#377 Desperate Cargo
#378 Death Run
#379 Deep Recon
#380 Silent Threat
#381 Killing Ground
#382 Threat Factor
#383 Raw Fury
#384 Cartel Clash
#385 Recovery Force
#386 Crucial Intercept
#387 Powder Burn
#388 Final Coup
#389 Deadly Command
#390 Toxic Terrain
#391 Enemy Agents
#392 Shadow Hunt
#393 Stand Down
#394 Trial by Fire

The Don Pendleton's Executioner®

TRIAL BY FIRE

TORONTO • NEW YORK • LONDON
AMSTERDAM • PARIS • SYDNEY • HAMBURG
STOCKHOLM • ATHENS • TOKYO • MILAN
MADRID • WARSAW • BUDAPEST • AUCKLAND

Recycling programs
for this product may
not exist in your area.

First edition September 2011

ISBN-13: 978-0-373-64394-3

Special thanks and acknowledgment to
Charles Rogers for his contribution to this work.

TRIAL BY FIRE

Printed in U.S.A.

A brave man may fall, but he cannot yield.

—Latin Proverb

When odds are stacked against you, and the enemy seems too big, stand up. Stand up and fight. It is might and heart that are the deciding factors in every great battle.

—Mack Bolan

THE MACK BOLAN LEGEND

Nothing less than a war could have fashioned the destiny of the man called Mack Bolan. Bolan earned the Executioner title in the jungle hell of Vietnam.

But this soldier also wore another name—Sergeant Mercy. He was so tagged because of the compassion he showed to wounded comrades-in-arms and Vietnamese civilians.

Mack Bolan's second tour of duty ended prematurely when he was given emergency leave to return home and bury his family, victims of the Mob. Then he declared a one-man war against the Mafia.

He confronted the Families head-on from coast to coast, and soon a hope of victory began to appear. But Bolan had broken society's every rule. That same society started gunning for this elusive warrior—to no avail.

So Bolan was offered amnesty to work within the system against terrorism. This time, as an employee of Uncle Sam, Bolan became Colonel John Phoenix. With a command center at Stony Man Farm in Virginia, he and his new allies—Able Team and Phoenix Force—waged relentless war on a new adversary: the KGB.

But when his one true love, April Rose, died at the hands of the Soviet terror machine, Bolan severed all ties with Establishment authority.

Now, after a lengthy lone-wolf struggle and much soul-searching, the Executioner has agreed to enter an "arm's-length" alliance with his government once more, reserving the right to pursue personal missions in his Everlasting War.

Democratic Republic of the Congo

The flight attendant screamed as the machete was brandished beneath her nose and recoiled against the fuselage. The men laughed unpleasantly. The captives cowered cross-legged with their wrists bound behind them beneath the remaining wing. The man with the machete dragged the tip of his blade down the woman's throat and let it rest on her collarbone. He grinned over his shoulder and said something choice to his confederates in Swahili. The men laughed again.

Mack Bolan, aka the Executioner, screwed the launcher-adapter onto the muzzle of his submachine gun and began his creep.

The Bombardier Challenger 604 jet lay in the little valley below like a stricken bird. This type of aircraft was classified as a heavy private jet. The twin-engine bird was configured to carry up to ten passengers in very swanky style. The smoldering scar in the 604's tail section said someone had salted its tail with a shoulder-launched surface-to-air missile.

The pilot had been good. It was obvious that he had crash-landed rather than crashed. He'd aimed for the little valley that opened up a slot in the jungle canopy and hit the creek that divided it like a runway. He'd lost his starboard wing on a tree, but the fuselage looked to be mostly intact. A heavy tree bough hung brutally speared through the cockpit in a way that looked like it had gone very badly for the pilot.

Bolan descended to the valley floor. He caught the unmistakable stench of burned human flesh.

Rescue missions were one of the soldier's least favorite activities. If the situation was bad enough to send him as the final option, the situation was just about FUBAR. Solo missions on foot in equatorial Africa in summertime were about as bad as rescue missions got. Among the host of all things FUBAR about this mission was the fact that all of his equipment had been begged, borrowed or stolen for him by the CIA station in Pretoria. By the same token it could have been worse. South Africans had a well-deserved reputation for solid kit. The old L42A1 "Enforcer" sniper rifle over Bolan's shoulder was a forty-year-old Pretoria police issue, but it was tough. The BXP submachine gun in Bolan's hand was the size of a large pistol and a cleaned up, optical-sighted version of the old US 1980s-era MAC-10.

An example of the BXP's more interesting features was that it was one of the few submachine guns that had ever been adapted to fire rifle grenades.

Bolan clicked a riot grenade onto the launching rings of his weapon as he came within one hundred yards of the situation.

He counted nine hostiles. They were Africans, but they wore no uniforms of any of the local armies within shouting distance. Most of them were armed with ChiCom AK knock-offs. The bad guys were at an extremely low state of alert and seemed to be in a jovial mood. While half were busy ransacking suitcases and carry-ons taken from the plane, the rest were watching what the man wielding the machete was going to do to the flight attendant next with avid and concupiscent interest.

Bolan counted ten captives. Eight were U.S. Military preparatory school cadets huddled in a line beneath the wing. The remaining two were crew. The flight attendant was in midassault, and a person who appeared to be the copilot lay off to one side and in very bad shape. As the soldier circled in, he found his assessment of the pilot's fate was correct. He had been killed in the crash, and the survivors had buried him. The invaders had exhumed the pilot's corpse, stripped it, emasculated it and pinned it upside down against the fuselage with tent spikes and burned it.

The flight attendant screamed as the man with the machete hacked off the pilot's hand. The corpse sagged on the three points still holding it in place. Machete man picked up the charred, fallen extremity and breathed over it like a man smelling pork chop that had just come out of the oven. The flight attendant crushed herself against the curve of the fuselage. Machete man raised his blade and pushed it hard enough between the woman's clavicles to draw blood. He shoved the severed hand beneath her nose and snarled. Bolan didn't speak Swahili but he was pretty sure the man had said "Eat!"

The man shoved the hand against the woman's face and shouted in English, "Eat!"

The other invaders laughed.

Bolan raised his BXP and fired.

The one-and-half-pound South African riot grenade hit the man in the side of the head at about eighty miles per hour. He dropped the machete and rubbernecked three steps sideways into the wing with the embedded grenade ejecting its multiple skip-chaser bomblets out of his skull like a slot machine paying off. Bolan wrenched the rifle-grenade rings off his weapon and spun the suppressor tube onto his smoking muzzle. Thick gray gas began to fill the camp like a fog.

Two men turned towards the sound of the grenade's launch-thump, but Bolan had already moved. The two men sprayed the underbrush on full-auto. Bolan put 3-round bursts through each man's chest and kept circling. South Africans knew something about riots, and the bomblets were filling the area with gas with remarkable efficiency. The jungle fighters had clearly never been exposed to CS. They stumbled about waving their arms and firing their guns in all directions. Two of the smarter ones turned their weapons on the captives. Bolan burned down both men before they could get off a shot.

A guerrilla caught sight of Bolan through his streaming eyes and charged, waving a *panga* and screaming hysterically. The Executioner's first burst staggered him, and the second sent him sprawling into the mud by the creek. The soldier kept circling. His weapon made a suppressed snapping noise, but between the gas, the screaming and AK full-auto fire the enemy still hadn't spotted him.

Two of the cadets jumped up to make a run for it.

"Cadets! Stay down!" Bolan roared.

They were teenagers, but they were U.S. Military teenagers and they were used to being bellowed at. The two cadets dropped like rocks. Bolan's yell had a wonderfully focusing effect on the remaining five guerrillas. They spun on their oppressor. The soldier knocked them down like bowling pins. The BXP racked open on a smoking empty chamber with two targets still standing. Bolan dropped the spent weapon and slapped leather for the South African police pistol on his belt. A rifle bullet cracked by his head far too close for comfort. Bolan double-tapped each assailant in the chest to cease hostilities and two more in the face to put them down.

The pistol racked open on empty. The screaming and shooting had stopped. The camp was quiet except for sobbing and choking, and the hiss of the CS munitions.

Bolan took a deep breath and strode into the gas.

He drew his knife and slashed the bonds of each cadet "Get out of the gas! Stick your heads in the creek! Go! Go! Go!" Bolan hooked the copilot under the arms. He had two broken legs, was gut-shot and the gas wasn't doing him any favors.

"You!" Bolan shouted at the flight attendant. "Help me!" Bolan dragged the copilot to the creek. Cadets lay prone in a line with their heads in the water like horses that had galloped a hundred miles.

Bolan lay the copilot down and grabbed a fallen canteen. He shoved it into the flight attendant's hands. "Wash out your eyes, then his!" Bolan stuck his head beneath the water and blinked repeatedly. He rose and reloaded his submachine gun and pistol, then scooped up a blood-spattered knit cap and strode back into the gas. He gathered up the still hissing gas bomblets and hurled them downstream.

The soldier went back to the crew and took a knee beside

the blonde flight attendant. Her eyes were red, swollen and still streaming from the gas. The copilot's inflamed eyes rolled with delirium. He moaned as the woman flushed them out. Her Boer accent was thick enough to cut with a knife. "His legs were broken in the crash."

"And after?"

"Bastards came at dawn. Pieter took a shot at them, didn't he, but he was hurt and missed. They shot him in the stomach, twice. Called him long pig. Said he was going to taste better if he died slow. Made us dig up the pilot." The woman shuddered. "Did some kind of voodoo with him."

Bolan gave the flight attendant a frank look. "You all right?"

"Yes, I mean, no, I mean, it was bad, but I'm not like you mean. I think they wanted to have more fun with us. But from the way they talked? They got a boss man, some fella called Caesar, and a boss woman, Mama-something. They're shite-scared of them." The woman nodded at the female cadet, and the rest as they worked. "Me, the girl? God help us, the boys? I think the boss man and his cronies get first crack."

"Stay with Pieter. We'll make a litter."

The cadets began to rise up from the creek. They milled around looking between the battlefield and Bolan as the remaining gas dispersed. The soldier glanced upward as he heard thunder roll. This neck of the rain forest was known to average eighty inches of rain per year, and the daily deluge was about to unload. They had to get moving. Bolan grimaced as he took in what had once been the cadets' mirror-bright, full dress uniform shoes. They would all be lame by nightfall.

"Lose the shoes!" The cadets gazed at him numbly. Bolan pointed at the corpses. "If you didn't pack boots or sneakers, you've got six pairs of boots and three pairs of sandals right there. Strip the bodies. Cut off the shirtsleeves and pant legs. If the boots are too big, wrap your feet until they fit." The cadets just stared. Bolan bellowed at the shell-shocked military cadets. "Move!"

A very large cadet wiped at his streaming eyes. He tottered

over to the nearest corpse and began tugging off its pants. He threw up but moved on to the shirt. Another cadet moved to help him. "Once you got your feet taken care of, take anything of use and pile it here," Bolan ordered. "Weapons, cell phones, matches, money, spare clothes, anything of value."

The soldier stuck his head in the cabin as two of the cadets went through it.

The interior had been ransacked in an inefficient fashion. Clothes and personal effects were scattered from the cockpit to the lavatory. The plane hadn't been stripped clean like the bones of a kill the way one might expect in Equatorial Africa. The looters had simply taken whatever they wanted rather than every last thing of value.

That didn't bode well.

Bolan walked over to the growing piles of plunder.

The weapons were nearly all Chinese Type 56 AK-47s with folding spike bayonets. The standouts were a Russian RPD machine gun and a Dragunov sniper rifle that was missing its telescopic sight. Bolan found two South African RAP-401 pistols like the one he carried, which likely belonged to the pilot and copilot, since machetes and *pangas* seemed to be the usual weapon of choice for the locals.

The loot from the plane was nearly as welcome as the firearms. Bolan had brought a first-aid kit, but the plane's kit was the kind of medical smorgasbord that only a private luxury craft that never expected to have a medical emergency insisted on including. This jet also had a survival kit.

The random pile included books of matches, several lighters, watches, cell phones and the personal effects of tribal militias.

Bolan frowned at the last and unfortunately smallest pile before him.

There was very little in the way of rations, and what there was consisted of three small bags of rice. The universal mess of irregular forces in sub-Saharan Africa was boiled rice and bush meat of the day. It was going to be Bolan and his squad's as well for the foreseeable future. What was missing told him a lot. There were no blankets. No sleeping bags or hammocks. All these men carried were their weapons and a light lunch. The fact that these men were so lightly outfitted told Bolan that they were a patrol, broken off from a much larger camp, not far away, and probably expected back for dinner. Someone was going to start wondering just where they had gotten to, and sooner than Bolan liked. He swiftly divvied up the piles into working loads and packed them into the luggage that had shoulder straps.

He nodded at the tallest and largest cadet as the youth laced up his commandeered boots. "You."

The young man leaped to his feet. "Sir?"

Bolan checked the load in the RPD. "You're my pig man."

"Sir?"

Bolan shoved the RPD into the young man's hands. "You're my pig man. You are humping this pig." Bolan draped two canvas sacks containing spare 100-round drums across the oxlike shoulders before him. "You copy?"

"Yes, sir."

"Who can shoot a pistol?"

A diminutive cadet and the flight attendant raised their hands. Bolan handed out South African steel to the woman and gave the cadet a rifle and spare magazines. "Who knows how to make a litter?"

A black cadet raised his hand.

"Good, grab a buddy and get the copilot loaded up."

Bolan looked at the dead enemies. Their tracks said they had come from the west. The creek was flowing south. "Put the bodies in the creek."

The cadets stared. They were close to losing it. "Move!" One advantage Bolan had on this mission was that his charges were U.S. Military preparatory school cadets. Unlike a lot of American teenagers, they knew how to take orders. "I have to make a call."

The cadets and crew all gave Bolan very hopeful looks

He walked a bit away and pressed a preset button on the CIA satellite phone he'd picked up in Pretoria. He waited while his signal moved through significant filters. Aaron "the Bear" Kurtzman answered. "Striker, this is Bear. Sitrep."

"Objectives were taken. I took them back. Pilot is dead. Copilot is badly injured and going septic."

"Describe 'taken,' Striker."

"Nine hostiles down. Believe hostiles happened upon crash site by chance. They're not our shooters, but they're not alone. They were a patrol for a larger force."

"Any identifiers?"

"Leaders possibly named Caesar and Mama. Check the scuttlebutt for the area."

"Copy that, Striker."

"Pilot died in crash. His body was exhumed. Things were done. I interrupted an atrocity in the making. I have a worst-case scenario. Requesting immediate extraction."

"Negative, Striker. No extraction assets within range."

"Requesting immediate backup. SEALs, Rangers, anyone within airborne range."

"Negative on U.S. Military personnel, Striker."

"Request Farm personnel, Able, Phoenix, any and all available."

"Negative on Farm personnel." Bolan could hear the regret in Kurtzman's voice. "Exposure is already too high."

The vault of the African heavens broke open. Rain sheeted down as if liquid curtains falling out of the sky. The silver lining was that maybe it would cover their tracks and help obscure the crime scene.

"Striker..."

Bolan knew by Kurtzman's voice it was bad. "Copy, Bear."

"I have been instructed to tell you that if you can extract the primary objective, secondary objectives can be considered... expendable."

Bolan's blood went cold. "I understand. Farm Protocol 4. Mission understood."

"Copy that, Striker. Will advise."

There was no Farm Protocol 4. It was a code word arranged by Bolan and Kurtzman. It could have been Corn Flakes or

Looks Like Rain. What Bolan had just told Kurtzman was that he had gone rogue. It was Bolan's mission, and he was operating outside government jurisdiction. No one was expendable save himself, and the Stony Man Farm computer expert should establish a private link between Bolan and the Farm.

"Any chance on a supply drop?"

"Working on it. Must advise not to plan on it."

"Copy that. Striker out."

Bolan strode back into the center of camp. "Everyone, take a gun. Take a pack. Take a machete." Bolan glanced up as the African sky continued to unload. "We're out of here."

2

“Dead!” Julius Caesar Segawa was incensed. As far as he was concerned, this section of the rain forest was his private reservation. Anything that entered was either prey or asked and paid for permission to enter. He stared down at the naked, bloated, bullet-perforated, logjam of his men clogging a bend in the creek. “Dead! I want them dead! Whoever has committed this atrocity! They burn in my fire! Their livers sizzle upon my plate with onions!”

Segawa’s men shook their rifles as they became willingly infected with their savior’s rage.

Solomon Obua knelt his mighty frame by the creek bed and stared at the bodies. Obua had been a Ugandan superheavyweight Olympic boxing contender. His dreams of Olympic and professional boxing glory had ended after he had killed his second opponent in the ring in his second Pan-African game. Obua had joined the army, and in the forest he had heard the call of Julius Caesar Segawa—his true calling. Years of jungle fighting had stripped Obua’s six-foot-six, 250 pound physique down to 210 pounds, which left him looking like a bodybuilder who had spent the last six months in a death camp. His body consisted of little else but muscle and sinew that crawled across his bones. Segawa’s men grew their hair and beards out to be more like Jesus, and Segawa, but Obua still shaved his head as he had when he was a boxer. Segawa ruled through religious intimidation and willpower. Obua enforced Segawa’s will through sheer physical intimidation.

Obua's father had been a game guide for safari hunters before Ugandan independence from the United Kingdom. There was nothing Obua didn't know about tracking in Equatorial Africa. It was Obua's belief that over the past ten years God had told him directly that his best quarry, and his best food, was man.

They had found the crash site, and what Obua had discovered there intrigued him. There had clearly been a mighty battle but no trace of any of the brethren. The rain had washed away much of the evidence, but throwing the bodies in the creek was simple deduction. Obua slid into the water and pulled a corpse to him. He stuck an inhumanly long and bony finger into a bullet hole and probed. A bullet came up beneath his ministrations. "A 9 mm round, Caesar. Subsonic hollowpoint." He turned to the next closest body and dug another mushroom-shaped bullet out his best scout's spleen. "Another 9 mm, subsonic hollowpoint."

Segawa's men had committed the worst atrocities that Africa had seen in the new century, yet several soldiers turned from the sight of Obua's hands-on crime-scene investigation and threw up. Obua probed every last injury of every corpse. William Wagaluka had been the squad leader. The burned and bone-crushed wound in the side of his head confounded even Obua. He pulled the bullets out of the last two bodies and peered at them. "More 9 mms…solids."

"Brother William said he had Uncle Sam's children in his grasp." Segawa mentally reviewed the pictures of the cowering cadets Wagaluka had texted him. The flight attendant would be given to the men. The female cadet had intrigued Segawa particularly. The single cell-phone picture he had seen of her had painted an entirely new ritual in his mind. "You say the Americans have reached out for their children so fast?"

Obua looked long and hard at a bloody bullet and then flicked it into the water. The more he examined the situation the more it intrigued him. "The Americans, they no use 9 mms except in their pistols. They all carbined up."

"English?" Segawa scowled. "French?"

"Same-same." Obua stared down into the face of one of the corpses. The eyes of the dead were usually flat and glassy as a fish's. Every brother's eyes were inflamed like blood-engorged golf balls. Obua pulled a body onto the bank. He leaned his huge hands on its belly and shoved. More men turned away in nausea and horror as Obua smelled what came out of the dead man's lungs. "Caesar?"

"Yes, brother."

"Our brothers were gassed."

"Gassed?"

"That is how he overcame nine of the brethren."

"He?"

"Yes."

"What do you tell me, Brother Obua?"

"I tell you the children of Uncle Sam were beneath your hand, and then Satan's child fell from the sky and took them back."

"One man?" Segawa looked askance at his most mighty of minions. "Truly, brother?"

"We saw nor heard no choppers. He must have jumped from a plane, from high above the clouds."

Segawa shook his braids and stared up through the rain at the unforgiving, Old Testament God who approved of the old ways. His men waited for Segawa to speak wisdom. "He came from the south."

Obua smiled. "Yes, brother."

"From South Africa, only from that benighted land could he have acquired his apparel of war, and a jet to speed him here."

"It makes perfect sense. He is some kind of mercenary, or commando."

"Sent by the begetters of these pale children of privilege."

"Expendable." Obua grinned. "Deniable."

"Alone," Segawa added.

"I have an idea. I think—"

"I know what you think, brother." Segawa stared unblinkingly up into the rain as if God on high seemed to beam him information. "You think of who would want to shoot down the plane. I ask you who hates the Americans most."

"The heathens who serve Mohammed."

"You think they will pay a pretty penny to have the children in their grasp."

Obua looked into the sky happily. "They would shower pennies upon us like the rain."

Segawa's head snapped around. His judging finger stabbed at Obua. "You cannot serve both God and mammon, brother!"

Obua cast his eyes down. "I thought of God's Army, brother, and our rebuilding." The fact was that the last open battle God's Army had fought with the Uganda People's Defence Force had gone rather badly. It was God's Army's intention to overthrow Uganda and establish paradise on Earth. At the moment, though, they found terrorizing pagan villages across the Democratic Republic of the Congo—DRC—border a safer and more profitable activity.

Segawa slowly lowered his finger. "I, too, think of our rebuilding, brother." He smiled unexpectedly. "I think of eight new recruits."

Obua straightened at the thought. "Yes, brother…"

"God's child-soldiers have served us so well." Segawa gestured at several of the men who had at one time been kidnapped from their villages as children and brutally adopted into God's Army. "But now they have grown so tall and strong!"

The men shook their weapons and shouted their allegiance.

Segawa turned his gaze heavenward once more. "Eight ghost-faced children of privilege! Striking down God's enemies! The children of the colonizers! Destroying the heirs of colonialism who spoil our sweet land! What shall our enemies make of it? What shall the world make of it? This is my vision." Segawa raised his hands and roared into the rain. "So let it be written! So let it be done!"

Obua leaned in while the men cheered wildly. "If what we surmise is true, then he must walk east to cross the Ugandan border."

"Uganda, our Promised Land," Segawa intoned. "Zion."

Religious fervor mixed with the sociopathic need to kill filled and inflamed Obua's belly. "The White Satan's servant marches with an army of children. He will be slow, Caesar."

"Then find him, brother. Find him."

"HALT!" BOLAN CALLED. The cadets sagged in place. The two cadets carrying the copilot lowered him to the ground. The flight attendant knelt and cradled Pieter's head in her lap. Bolan glanced at the sun. They had route marched for four hours. The rain had stopped. The sun was sinking and turning orange. "Everybody line up, I want—"

A cadet shook his head and rubbed his wrists. "Man, who are you? Where the hell are the helicopters? Where're—"

Bolan roared at parade-ground decibels. He would have exactly one opportunity to weld these young men and women into a unit. It was their only chance for survival. "Line up for inspection!"

The eight military cadets snapped into line and to attention as if Bolan had cracked a whip. The Executioner rounded on the questioning cadet. "What is your name, Cadet?" It was embroidered on the front of the young man's uniform jacket, but Bolan demanded it anyway.

"Jovich, Sir! Martin—"

"Don't you 'sir' me, Jock-itch! I made sergeant back in the day! I worked for a living and I still do!"

"Yes, Sergeant!"

The next cadet in line snickered. "Jock-itch…"

Bolan stepped in front of the sneering youth. He didn't like what he saw. The tall blond cadet was too handsome for his own good and knew it. He stank just a bit of an excess of privilege and a distinct lack of discipline. Unfortunately, he was priority number one, and Bolan knew there was a very good chance that he was going to die for this egotistical cadet. "You got a name?"

The cadet mockingly looked at the front of his tunic. A

vague Southern drawl inflected his insolence. "Yeah, Metard, John."

Bolan smiled. "Full name?"

The cadet bristled. He looked Bolan in the eye and what he saw there snapped his eyes front once more. "Metard…Jean-Marie."

"Thank you, Meatwad."

Metard clenched his jaw but kept his retort behind his teeth. Mirth was visibly suppressed up and down the line. Bolan wasn't surprised to find that Metard wasn't well-liked by his fellow cadets. The soldier moved down the line and looked at another blond cadet. He was shorter than Metard, but even at fifteen years of age he had the shoulders of an Olympic swimmer. The cadet grinned and stood at perfect attention. "Eischen, Alexander Charles, Sergeant!"

Bolan raised one eyebrow slightly. "Felt the need to sneak that Charles in on me, did you?"

Eischen slid a hostile eye towards Metard. "It's no Jean-Marie, Sergeant, but we do our best."

Bolan liked Eischen's attitude. "Alexander Charles Eischen, fine. Ace it is."

The female cadet standing next to Eischen gave him an approving look. Bolan stepped up to the lone female in the group. She had dark hair, dark eyes and an olive complexion. She squared her shoulders as she fell under Bolan's scrutiny. "Shelby, Sergeant! Maria Dirazar!"

Bolan's eyes narrowed in thought. "Shelby…"

"Most people just call me Shel–"

Bolan lunged in eyeball to eyeball. "Do I look like most people to you, Cadet?"

"No, Sergeant!" Shelby went to ramrod attention. "You are like no man I have ever met!"

"Good answer, Snake."

Shelby blinked. "Snake, Sergeant?"

"Shelby. Carroll Shelby. Greatest American car designer of the twentieth century. You've heard of the Cobra? Super

Cobra? Super Snake?" Bolan shook his head with weariness. "You're Snake, Cadet."

Shelby's whisper followed Bolan as he walked down the line. "Sweet…"

Bolan found himself in front of a fifteen-year-old youth who could look him in the eye. The young, lantern-jawed mesomorph in the making stared straight ahead with a grim look on his face. Bolan looked long and hard at the name embroidered on the front of the young man's uniform.

Hudjak.

"Cadet?"

"Yes, Sergeant." The tall young man was a tower of stoicism.

"I think we'll just call you Huge."

"Yes, Sergeant."

"Until you screw up, Huge."

"Yes, Sergeant."

Next cadet in line was the only black cadet. Except for Huge, he was the biggest in the group. Bolan read his tag. "Johnson."

"Yes, Sergeant. John Henry."

"You know the legend of the man you were named after, Cadet?"

"Heard it every day growing up, Sergeant. Told every day it was something I'd better live up to."

Bolan smelled leadership potential. "Good to know, Hammer."

Hudjak elbowed Johnson in congratulations as Bolan moved on.

A young Chinese man stood at attention. "King, Donald, Sergeant!" The cadet's voice dropped low. "Sergeant?"

Bolan dropped his voice in return. "Cadet?"

"Sergeant, please don't call me Donkey Kong. It takes a fistfight every year at the start of school to scrape that one off."

"I wouldn't do that to you, Cadet. We'll keep it Don King."

The cadet looked confusedly for the rub. “But, Sergeant, that’s my name.”

“Don King,” Bolan prompted. “The Rumble in the Jungle? The Thrilla in Manila?”

Cadet King stared at Bolan vacantly.

“The Sign from God hairstyle?” Bolan tried. He was becoming painfully aware of the fact that it had been some time since he had spent any quality time with the latest generation of America. “Fine, what’s your real name?”

“Sergeant?”

“You’re second-generation Chinese.”

“Yes, Sergeant. My parents came from Taiwan.”

“So ‘Donald’ is the American name they picked for you. Chinese put the family name first and the given second. That makes your family name King. What’s your real name, Cadet?”

The cadet sighed painfully. “Dong, Sergeant.”

“Donger, I tried to be merciful.”

Cadet King rolled his eyes. “I knew it.”

Bolan lunged. “I will roll your eyes right out of your head, Donger!”

Cadet King snapped to attention. “Cadet Donger! Ready for duty, Sergeant!”

Bolan came to the last cadet in line. If he hadn’t looked down, he might have missed him. The cadet was clearly Indian or Pakistani. The young man just cracked five foot two, and if he was more than ninety-eight pounds dripping wet Bolan would be surprised. He read the young man’s moniker.

The cadet just barely kept his shoulders from sagging.

Bolan heard Metard snicker back in line and made a note of it.

For the moment the soldier looked at the cadet before him with a modicum of sympathy. “Son of the Indian subcontinent?”

“Technically I was born in California, Sergeant, but we went back to West Bengal right after for five years for my father’s job. Then we came back again.”

"Lovely country," Bolan opined. "Been there several times."

"Thank you, Sergeant. My family goes back to visit every year."

"Well," Bolan mused. "Might as well get this over with."

The young man nodded bravely. "Yes, Sergeant."

Bolan read the embroidery again—Rudipu.

"Hell of a handle," Bolan admitted.

"Yes, Sergeant. Thank you."

"You got a first name, Cadet?"

"Gupti, Sergeant."

Metard snickered again. The young man was digging a deeper hole for himself. Bolan stayed with the business at hand. "Gupti Rudipu." Bolan nodded. "Hell of a handle."

"Yes, Sergeant."

"You know the possibilities are mind-boggling."

"Yes, Sergeant. I know."

"I bet you do. Any mitigating factors before I pass judgment, Cadet?"

The teenaged cadet considered his résumé. "Well, I am captain of the rifle team at the academy."

Bolan perked an eyebrow. "NRA Whistler Boy High-Power Junior Team Match?"

The sack of chicken bones Cadet Rudipu called a chest swelled with pride. "This will be my second year, Sergeant."

Bolan nodded. "Never met a rifleman I didn't like, Rude."

Rudipu beamed. "Yes, Sergeant! Thank you, Sergeant! I'll make you proud of me, Sergeant! I promise I will!"

"No one likes the squad cocksucker, Rude."

Rudipu snapped back to attention. "No, Sergeant!"

Bolan turned back to face the line. "All right, I want—"

"Hey!" Metard's outrage boiled over. "How come everyone else gets cool names and me and Jovich's suck?"

King held his peace on that one. Jovich stepped away from Metard like he was radioactive.

Bolan rounded on Metard. "Because they know when to have themselves a tall frosty STFU when certain others I can name ran their mouths."

Metard's face flushed scarlet.

Bolan regarded the cadet like something he had just scraped off his shoe. "You want another nickname, Meatwad? You earn it. You read me?"

Metard shook with impotent rage.

"I asked you a question!" Bolan bellowed.

"Yes, Sergeant!"

"Yes, what?"

"I read you, Sergeant!"

Bolan took a few steps back and eyed his squad. "You have questions. Let me answer ninety percent of them right now. I am the angry god of your universe. You will do what I say when I say it. You are cadets, in training to become officers in the United States Army, Navy, Air Force and Marines. I expect you to act like it. Do those two things, and you might just live through this. I hope that clears things up."

The eight cadets stared at Bolan in a mixture of shock and awe.

Bolan glanced up at the sinking sun. "We need to do distance, but given the nature of the situation, I am going to allow each of you to ask me one question, once. After that, every last question had better be pertinent and about survival. Now. Go."

The cadets glanced around at one another. Johnson raised his hand.

"This isn't the classroom, Hammer. We're in the jungle. We don't raise our hands. We don't have the time."

Johnson nodded. "Sorry, Sarge, I just—" Johnson suddenly balked at his own temerity. "I mean, may I call you Sarge, Sergeant?"

"If it'll speed things up."

Johnson gazed on Metard with cold pleasure. "Well, I don't want a new nickname or anything, Sarge, but I'm with Meatwad. I mean, what's going on? Don't get me wrong, you are *super*-bad, but, like, where are the choppers and Navy SEALs and shit?"

"There are no choppers. There are no Navy SEALs and shit. There are no carriers or special operations teams currently in range. Don't hold your breath waiting for them. All you have is each other and me."

Jovich eyed Bolan warily.

"You got something to say Jock-itch?" Bolan asked.

"We're American citizens. Our plane got shot down. I mean, why isn't anyone coming?"

Bolan looked around the squad. "Anyone know why not?"

It was Johnson who spoke. "Because all modern U.S. administrations have had a reluctance to have American soldiers shooting black Africans."

Bolan nodded. "And?"

"And neither the Democratic Republic of the Congo, Uganda, Sudan or anyone else has authorized the United States to send military flights over their airspace, much less Egypt, Libya or any other North African countries, and the DRC sure as hell hasn't given Uncle Sam permission to mount a military rescue mission within its borders."

"You just made squad leader, Hammer."

Johnson seemed to have mixed emotions about the promotion. "Thanks, Sarge."

Eischen gave Bolan an appraising look. "So, who are you?"

"I don't know, Ace, you tell me."

Cadet Eischen continued to maintain his positive attitude. "Expendable, deniable and…super-bad?"

"Something like that."

The truth was dawning on Metard. "So who sent you?"

"You tell me."

Cadet Shelby addressed the five-hundred-pound gorilla in the camp. "He's here because you're the son of a United States senator, Meatwad."

Metard reappraised Bolan. "My father sent you?"

Bolan locked eyes with the prize. "I wasn't sent. I was begged."

Metard flinched.

"Your father is a senior United States senator and a war hero. When you went missing, he called in every marker he had. Then he begged the President of the United States—your soon-to-be commander in chief, assuming you live that long—for his son's life. The powers that be begged me. I said yes."

Metard cast his eyes down.

Hudjak frowned. "So if there are no carriers in range, where did you come from?"

"Where do you think?"

"You parachuted in."

"You think?"

"From where?"

Bolan gave the hulking cadet a pointed look.

"South Africa?"

Bolan nodded.

"Why were you in South Africa?"

"That's three questions, Huge."

Cadet Hudjak smiled. "Sorry, Sarge. I beg forgiveness and ask that my multiple questions not impose on Snake's rights of inquiry."

Shelby gave the guy a winning smile.

"Forgiven. You got a question, Snake?"

"So we're walking out of here, Sarge?"

"That is the long and short of it."

Visible alarm spread down the line. King almost raised his hand and stopped himself. "Sarge?"

"Donger?"

"What happened?"

"You tell me."

King did some math. "Terrorists figured out that the son of a U.S. senator was on a private flight to an international military leadership seminar in South Africa. They decided to shoot us down."

"Look at him go," Bolan said.

"And those…guys—" King shuddered "—who found us are not them. Who were they?"

Shelby spoke quietly. "I did a paper on the Congo Wars last quarter. Those guys were tribal militia, rebels…or worse."

"Last call." Bolan looked up and down the group. "Anyone else?"

Rudipu perked up. "Sarge?"

"Rude?"

"Do you always answer a question with a question?"

The ghost of a smile passed across Bolan's face. "No."

A few nervous laughs broke out. "Cold camp tonight. I don't want any fires giving us away. Divvy up the food from the plane. Sandwiches, power bars, whatever snacks you brought with you. Eat half now, save the rest for breakfast. Long day tomorrow, and we're going to have to start catching whatever we eat real soon."

Bolan turned before a new round of questions started and went over to the crew. The copilot was in bad shape. His broken legs were swollen and smelled. There was nothing to be done about the bullets in his guts. "How's he doing?"

The flight attendant just managed to choke back a sob.

The copilot opened red-rimmed eyes. They were lucid as he surveyed Bolan. He spoke in about the thickest Australian drawl Bolan had ever heard. "Heard your palaver with the kids, then. Reckon you got a nickname for me, too?"

Bolan gave the dying man a grin. "You prefer Bullet-stop or Brittle-bones?"

The copilot grimaced good-naturedly as a rale passed through his lungs, "You know it hurts when I laugh, then."

The flight attendant mopped the bloody spittle from the copilot's mouth. "And me? Do I get a name, too?"

"What is your name?"

The woman looked steadily into Bolan's eyes. "Roos von Kwakkenbos."

"The Rudester has nothing on you, and you and Hudjak may be related."

Von Kwakkenbos laughed. "And?"

"We're just going to stick with Blondie." Bolan turned his attention back to the copilot. "How you doing?"

The copilot turned to Von Kwakkenbos. "Reckon you should take a look at the kids, get some tucker while the getting is good."

The woman gave the copilot a long look and went to join the cadets.

Copilot Pieter Llewellyn sighed, and there was a bad gurgle at the end of it. "Reckon I'm done, then. It's at least 150 klicks to the border."

"The cadets are willing to carry you. So am I."

"Fine bunch of lads. 'Preciate it. But those dipsticks following us? You're not going to beat them in a footrace, specially toting my carcass about. 'Sides, we both know I'm gonna cark it long before we ever reach Uganda. Guess there's nothing to be done."

"I could give you some more morphine," Bolan countered.

The copilot perked up. "Aw, that'd be bonzer, mate!"

Bolan readied an injector from the plane's kit. "You know, you're the only Australian I know who actually uses that word."

"Well, then, you've never been to Maralinga, then, have you? There's an—" Pieter's eyes just about rolled back in his head as the morphine flooded his veins. "Aww, beauty..."

"Would you believe me if I said I had?" Bolan asked.

"Believe almost anything you tell me at the moment."

"You saw what they did to the pilot."

Pieter's eyes hardened through the morphine haze. "Bill was always a bit of an asshole, but he didn't deserve that."

"Listen, if we bury you, they're most likely going to dig you up."

"Well, that'll waste a little of their time, then, won't it?" Pieter asked.

"Yeah, but then they'll probably eat you."

"Hope they choke." Pieter grinned past his bloody teeth. "Or at least get indigestion."

Bolan smiled. The copilot was a brave man.

"Well, your choice, then, mate. Burn me, bury me, leave me for the dipsticks. Reckon I'm fine with any of it."

"Mighty reasonable of you, Pieter." Bolan nodded. "How would you feel about all three?"

Arua, Uganda

Alireza Rhage looked out of his office window across the sea of lights just outside Arua proper. The constellations of campfires were a cosmos of misery. The twinkling lights were the result of thousands of refugees burning whatever flammable garbage they could find. Arua was swollen with those who had fled the internecine fighting in the Democratic Republic of the Congo and Sudan. The refugee camps were swiftly becoming suburban shantytowns rife with violence and despair.

They were fertile recruiting grounds.

Ostensibly Rhage was a businessman investing in Uganda's northern tea cultivation. Years of corruption and warfare had turned that industry into a shadow of what it once was. In his year and a half as a tea exporter, agricultural attaché Rhage had never turned a dime of profit. That was of no consequence. In reality, Captain Rhage was an exporter, and what he exported had reaped untold dividends in blood and human misery.

Rhage turned to his personal secretary. "You say there has been no report of a crash, and Flight 499 never arrived at Wonderboom Airport in Pretoria?"

Sergeant Major Pakzad shook his head. "No, Captain."

"Have there been any reported emergency landings?"

"There have been seven emergency landings by private

planes reported in sub-Saharan Africa within Flight 499's flight window, Captain, but none was reported by Flight 499."

"Given the nature of the emergency, could they have landed under false identification?"

"That is possible, of course, but none of the emergency landings recorded in the last forty-eight hours were made within reasonable distance of Flight 499's flight path."

"Does it strike you as odd, Sergeant Major, that a private flight full of American military cadets, one of them the son of a United States senator, appears to have disappeared without a trace?"

Pakzad smiled with pride. "Well, Captain. We did shoot it down."

Rhage smiled in return. It had been Sergeant Major Pakzad's plan. He was a brilliant intelligence officer. He and his staff constantly processed information and devised scenarios. In the sergeant major's fertile mind, Flight 499 and its passengers had gone from a nonactionable item of mild interest to an opportunity. "Yet, no international outcry. No rescue or salvage mission mounted that we know of. What does that tell you?"

"It says that perhaps the crash occurred in a place the United States cannot easily reach. A bad place, where they have no assets. So they are keeping the situation quiet."

"Which implies that the cadets may be alive."

"It is possible, given the nature of the emergency, the pilots did not get out a distress call. By the same token, it is possible that the United States has the power to suppress the situation. My best guess is that the plane crash-landed. If there are survivors they most likely used their cell phones to call for help, which we could not monitor or intercept. The United States has no realistic way to project force into the Congo, much less do so without creating an international incident. The northeastern corner of the DRC is one of the most violent, lawless places on Earth. The United States would not want to advertise they are missing people in the region. Any number of groups hostile to them could retrieve the survivors. A hostage situation involving U.S. military school cadets in Equatorial Africa would be a worst-case scenario for them."

Rhage glanced at the tri-corner border region of Sudan, Uganda and the DRC. "The best they could immediately manage would be to drop in Special Forces operators."

"Yes, but from where?" Pakzad pondered. "The United States? Divert them from operations in Afghanistan?"

"Nevertheless, I am taking this continuing silence to mean the Americans are up to something."

"Very well, Captain. Let us assume the Americans have somehow dropped in a rescue team. That leaves them trying to walk out of the Congo. In that case, their best option would be to make for the Ugandan border."

The corner of Rhage's mouth quirked up. Pakzad's plan was growing more momentous by the minute. "Straight toward us."

"Yes, Captain, and if you are correct, then I suspect the CIA station in Kampala is quietly arranging a team to meet them."

"I want you to quietly assemble a team of our own, and we will need native trackers who know the area."

"Yes, Captain!" Pakzad smiled. "We shall herd the little ducks and then pluck them!"

"You are confident, Sergeant Major. You are aware of the fact that U.S. Special Forces operatives are the best in the world."

"Yes, Captain. Yet I doubt they could have mustered a full Delta Force team, and they will be saddled with children."

"Military students, Sergeant Major."

"American teenagers," Pakzad scoffed. "Soft cadets."

Rhage smiled tolerantly. "Did you know that I attended academy in my youth?"

"No, Captain. I did not."

"Oh, I will admit, the greater proportion of my youthful studies stressed the glory of the Revolution and utter loyalty. Nevertheless, it was at academy where I first learned to read a map, use a compass, route march, and fire and field strip an automatic rifle."

"Yes, Captain. I understand," Pakzad's smile suddenly turned sly. It was a smile Rhage knew all too well, and it always meant something was afoot in the man's mind. "Captain?"

"Yes, Sergeant Major."

"I have an idea."

"I look forward very much to hearing it."

"I am reminded of the siege of Troy…"

THE CADETS SQUATTED in the morning mist and made a cold and meager breakfast of the individually wrapped cress-and-cucumber finger sandwiches that they'd despised during the flight, the few packs of peanuts and remaining odds and ends. The cadets had changed out of their dress uniforms and wore the T-shirts and shorts or casual pants they had packed for South Africa. Jovich eyed his tiny sandwich that consisted mostly of leaves. "Man, who is that guy, Rambo?"

Cadet Shelby ate the last honey-roasted peanut. "Sarge rocks." She carefully opened the empty foil pack like a letter and licked the salt and dust from the inside.

Metard and King immediately followed her lead and began licking foil.

Jovich shoved his sandwich into his mouth and glanced around to see if the sergeant was lurking. "And what's with the fraternity pledge names?"

Johnson licked mayonnaise off his fingers. "Actually, I kind of liked it when he went all *Heartbreak Ridge* on us."

Eischen took a swallow from the last can of Coke and passed it on. His eyes narrowed slyly. "He's taking a ragtag band of pubescent cadets and turning them into a well-oiled fighting machine."

Several cadets laughed. Rudipu eyed the battered ladder-sight of his Kalashnikov dubiously. "Man, I sure hope so."

Bolan appeared out of the mist with the plane's emergency folding shovel in hand. "Grave detail. Fall in."

The cadets stared as a unit. "Sarge?" Johnson asked.

"The first officer died around 4:00 a.m. last night. Follow me."

The cadets stared around at one another glumly. They rose and followed Bolan a little way through the trees. The copilot lay in an open grave about five feet deep and just long and wide enough to fit his frame. Miss von Kwakkenbos knelt beside the grave weeping. The copilot lay with his arms crossed over his chest holding his uniform cap. He looked at peace.

"I dug his grave, but he was your first officer. He was part of your flight. Flight 499. I figured you might want to cover him. Maybe say something over him."

Hudjak took the shovel from Bolan's hand without a word. He stood over the grave for a moment and then looked back at Bolan. "Sarge?"

"Huge?"

"They're just going to dig him up, and do him voodoo-style like they did the captain. Probably going to eat him."

"You're right, Huge." Bolan nodded. "Can anyone tell me why that doesn't matter?"

"Because there's nothing we can do about it." Shelby looked down at the dead copilot. "It doesn't matter what they do. What matters is what we do, and we respect our fallen."

Hudjak nodded and began shoveling.

The cadets watched silently as Flight 499's first officer went beneath the ground. "Hey," Metard said. "Huge."

The young man didn't look up from his work. "What do you want, Meatwad?"

"A turn."

Hudjak straightened. He gave Metard a look and handed over the entrenching tool. One by one each cadet took a turn burying their flight officer. Rudipu spent long moments patting the grave flat and even.

Bolan nodded. "Anyone want to say anything?"

Rudipu smiled and wiped the sweat from his brow. "He called me Sprout." A few of the cadets laughed quietly or smiled. Rudipu wiped tears from his face as he gazed upon the grave. "But he gave me a tour of the cockpit before we took off. He showed me his gun."

Shelby sniffed and pushed at her face. "He called me Sheila. When I said I was Air Force, he said he liked lady pilots. I liked him."

"He fought them." Johnson stared long and hard at the grave. "Even with two broken legs. He fought them."

Tears spilled down Cadet Eischen's cheeks. "Even when we didn't."

The cadets lowered their heads.

Bolan spoke over the grave. "He was Pieter Llewellyn, Lieutenant. He flew 604s for the Royal Australian Air Force, Transport Wing. He was honorably discharged after two enlistments and became a private contractor, specializing in the African VIP hub. He fought that plane to the ground." Bolan looked around at the survivors of Flight 499. "He said you were a likeable bunch of lads and sheilas. He said he'd brought you down, but it was up to me to keep you safe. He said take care of his Niners. He said take them home."

The cadets nodded at Bolan, who shook his head. "I couldn't promise him that."

The squad stared.

"I can only promise you two things. I leave no one behind, and I'll die before I let any of you get taken again."

Profound silence filled the gravesite.

"Flight Officer Llewellyn," Bolan intoned. "Niner Squad! Salute!"

The cadets saluted their fallen copilot with parade-ground precision.

"Fall out," Bolan ordered. "Gear up. Line up for inspection in one minute." The cadets and Von Kwakkenbos fell out and grabbed their kit. They were armed and in line in fifty seconds.

Bolan took Johnson's AK. "How many of you have fired a gun?"

Rudipu, Metard, Eischen and Von Kwakkenbos raised their hands.

"How many have fired an AK?"

All hands dropped.

"This is a Kalashnikov." Bolan swiftly ran through the manual of arms. "This is your selector lever." He pushed the lever through the settings, "Safe. Rock 'n' roll. Semiautomatic. These are your sights. They graduate from 100 to 800 meters. This is the fixed battle setting for all ranges up to 300 meters. This is your folding bayonet." The squad members eyes widened as Bolan snapped out the foot-long, quadrangular spike. Bolan snapped it back and returned the weapon to Johnson.

"Set your sights to fixed battle setting. Set your selectors to semiauto. You will not change these settings without permission. Unless the enemy is directly engaging you, you will not fire without permission. Our ammo supply is extremely limited. Every shot has to count. Some of the weapons have folding stocks. You will keep them deployed at all times. You will not fix bayonets unless you are out of ammunition or I have ordered you to do so. Does everyone understand?"

"Yes, sergeant!" the squad said in unison.

"Huge."

"Yes, Sergeant?"

"I have no time to train you. You're going to have learn the joys of supporting fire on the fly." Bolan pointed at the light machine gun Huge cradled. "Don't go Rambo on me. Use your bipod. Get on and off the trigger fast. Short bursts."

"Short bursts." Huge nodded. "Yes, Sergeant."

"Rude."

"Yes, Sergeant."

"So you're a rifleman."

"Yes, Sergeant."

Bolan eyed the Dragunov sniper rifle Metard was holding. "Switch with Meat."

Metard noted the "wad" suffix had been left off his name and smiled. "But Sarge, it's bigger than he is."

"He's just going to have to grow into it," Bolan said, as Rudipu took the Dragunov. The four-foot-long, nine and a half pound rifle nearly reached his chin. Bolan gave the cadet a meaningful look. "Fast."

Bolan looked at several abandoned dress uniforms. "Uncle

Sam still makes his full dress uniforms out of wool, Niners. You're going to want those jackets and slacks when it gets cold."

King glanced about as the morning mist turned to rainbowing steam in the morning sun. "Sarge?"

"Donger."

"Where does it get cold around here?"

Bolan pointed directly west at the mist-shrouded peaks that lay between the Niner squad and the Ugandan border. "There."

4

“What have you got for me, Bear?” Bolan asked. Kurtzman looked at his bank of monitors. One screen was devoted to the weather over Equatorial Africa. Three more coordinated satellite feeds as high-resolution imagery intelligence birds became available. Another screen was coordinated with signals intelligence satellites that were eavesdropping on the region. The largest screen, the one directly in front of Kurtzman, was dedicated to what he considered the “footwork” of the Computer Room—his own research and information processing.

“I have Julius Caesar Segawa.”

“Cute,” Bolan replied.

“Nothing cute about him.” Kurtzman looked at the only known photograph of the madman. With his knit cap, dreads and beard, Segawa could have passed for a reggae singer, except that reggae singers didn’t pose for portraits holding an automatic weapon while sitting on a pile of human heads. “We have very little confirmed on this guy, Striker, but what we do know is bad, and I mean bad.”

“This Caesar, he’s Lord’s Resistance Army?”

“Worse.”

“What does that mean?”

Kurtzman looked Segawa’s picture again. The Lord’s Resistance Army had been engaged in armed rebellion against the Ugandan government more or less since 1987. They believed in a heady blend of traditional African religion, spirit-medium mysticism and Apocalyptic Christianity. Kurtzman knew that the group certainly was not the first to use murder, abduction, rape, mutilation and sexual enslavement against civilian populations, but they had gone at it with an enthusiasm unseen in the twentieth century, and it is thought they had pioneered the use of child-soldiers in African conflicts.

"It seems Segawa got kicked out for going too far in his atrocities."

"Isn't that kind of like getting thrown out of a rock band for doing too many drugs, Bear?"

"Yeah, well, imagine if the lead singer started eating people." Kurtzman smiled in spite of himself. "You yourself told me you have firsthand evidence of the cannibalism thing here on the ground."

"I've seen firsthand that they eat hands. What else do we know?"

"Not much. Segawa split off and formed his own group called God's Army. They haven't had much success taking over the Lord's Resistance Army, much less overthrowing the Ugandan government. They pulled a big fade into Congo a few years back and have been under the radar ever since. All I can find are second- and thirdhand horror stories about them that missionaries and aid workers have heard from refugees."

"Anything pertinent?"

"He's supposed to have some woman with him. A witch doctor. Rumor is people in the region are even more scared of her than him." Kurtzman stared at the image of Segawa sitting on heads. "To be honest? I'm worried. I don't think he'll stop at just holding those kids for ransom. God only knows what he'll do."

"Any idea of their troop strength?"

"Depending who you listen to the Lord's Resistance Army has an estimated strength of fifteen hundred to three thousand men at any given time. Caesar and his God's Army are a splinter group and have been in the bush for several years. They're strong enough to raid villages with impunity, but in recent years they've been strictly avoiding the militaries on both sides of the border as well as their former brethren. I'd say Caesar's got to have at least one platoon. Possibly two."

The math was ugly. Bolan and his little troop were outnumbered by at least five if not possibly ten to one. Bolan changed the subject. "Any clue on our shooters?"

"That is something of a poser. All we have to go on are the photos of the plane you sent and the location of the crash site itself. Walking it backward from the crash site, the air defense guys I spoke with figure Flight 499 was probably at cruising altitude. For a Challenger 604 max is about forty-one thousand feet. Flight 499 would have been well below that, and given the prevailing weather maybe half that or less, but certainly well out of range of anything shoulder-launched. Going by the pictures, put together the damage to the plane and the pilots' ability to land it, our best guess is that 499 took a near miss by something using a proximity fuse. I'm thinking something vehicle-launched."

"More likely towed," Bolan surmised. "You got any probable launch sites?"

"Hard to imagine it was actually fired from the DRC. There just isn't anything in your neck of the woods with that kind of range. Best bet would be a launch from the northeastern extreme of Uganda or the southern tip of Sudan, but they would have had to have been very close to 499's flight path. We're talking right under it. The other two things of interest are that the only air defense weapons the Ugandans have are obsolete Russian antiaircraft guns. But the Sudanese do have a few Russian SA-2 Guideline missile batteries. Those could have reached out and touched Flight 499."

"But the few they have are all tasked with defending the capital and their air bases, they're all out of range of Flight 499's flight path, and even the yahoos in Khartoum aren't dumb enough to start firing at commercial flights, particularly ones with a U.S. senator's son aboard."

"That's how I see it, too, which leaves us with players we don't know about misbehaving in the tri-border region. Though it's hard to imagine any bad guys I can think of planning this operation. The logistics are too extreme to match the target."

"It wasn't planned. Our players were misbehaving as you said, but Flight 499 came up as a target of opportunity." Bolan's voice went cold. "And since we have unknown enemies playing with surface-to-air missiles in the area, I'm not going to get my resupply flight, am I?"

"Resupply is currently considered too dangerous. If the bad guys have access to medium range surface-to-air missiles, we must assume they have shoulder-launched weapons as well and may be moving into your area. How are your supplies?"

"On average everyone has four loaded magazines. We've got three pints of rice and some sandwich spread. After that we go directly to eating endangered animals."

Kurtzman scrolled the files on the cadets and the flight attendant. "How are your people holding up?"

Bolan's voice brightened. "Good, better than I'd expected. Pieter was right, they're a good bunch of lads and sheilas."

"So what is your current plan?"

"We keep heading west."

"I don't know if you can out march these guys, Striker."

"I know."

"So what are you going to do?"

"I'm going to reach out and show Caesar the Ides of March are upon him. Striker out."

BOLAN SCANNED THE SKIES as he clicked off. The daily downpour was just about due. "Rude! Hammer!" he called. "On me."

Cadets Johnson and Rudipu ran up and snapped to attention front and center. "Sarge?" Johnson asked.

"Squad leader, rumor is you intend to be a Marine."

"Yes, Sergeant. I hope to be Force Recon, like my father."

Bolan held out his compass and his spare map. "You know how to use these?"

"Yes, Sergeant."

"You're going to take Niner Squad straight up that mountain. If you push hard, you should be able to summit before dark."

"Yes, Sergeant."

"You're keeping a cold camp. I've had one of the bags of rice soaking in water since this morning in a plastic bag. Ace is carrying it, but he doesn't know it yet. It should be edible by the time you hit the top. Don't tell anybody, but Blondie has peanut butter and jelly. Tonight everyone in the squad gets a cup of rice and three tablespoons of the PB and J. Blondie will provision it out. Meat is carrying the second rice bag. You will put it in the plastic bag Ace is carrying and soak it overnight. If Rude and I are not back by morning, that and the other half of the peanut butter are breakfast and dinner. If we're still not back, you soak bag number three and continue to head due west."

"Yes, Sergeant."

"You will not engage the enemy unless you are attacked. Escape and evade. If you come across a village, do not make contact. They may be hostile. Even if they aren't, if they take you in, it could be a death sentence for them. Mark the position on the map and continue on."

"Yes, Sergeant."

Bolan handed Johnson one of the collected cell phones and five batteries. "I've put two presets at the top of the contact list. Number one is SARGE and number two is BEAR. Do not call out unless you're being attacked or run into unforeseen difficulties. If I am not back by tomorrow, call preset SARGE. If I do not respond, call preset BEAR. Do not answer any incoming calls unless the Caller ID says SARGE or BEAR. If you receive a call from BEAR at any time and I'm not here, you do anything and everything the Bear tells you. Got it?"

"Copy that, Sarge."

"You may hear gunfire. You'll probably see smoke. Remember the enemy likes to spray and pray. Single shots are probably me or Rude." Bolan looked into the earnest young cadet's face and saw doubt and fear. It was Johnson's first command, at age seventeen, in the jungles of Africa. "Hammer?"

"Sarge?"

Bolan knew from long experience that there was something about cold steel that braced backbones. "Have the men fix bayonets."

Johnson snapped his steel in place. "Yes, Sergeant!" The cadet frowned. "How are you going to catch up?"

"You'll be cutting the trail for us, Hammer."

"But won't the enemy find it, too?"

"Hammer, I'm counting on it."

Johnson grinned. "Copy that!"

Bolan clapped Johnson on the shoulder. "You have your orders, Squad Leader. Inform the team and get them moving. I will rendezvous within twenty-four to forty-eight hours."

"Yes, Sergeant." Johnson jogged back to the group. "Niner Squad! On me!"

Bolan turned to Rudipu as Johnson shouted in a decent imitation of a drill sergeant. "Fix bayonets!"

Bolan spoke quietly over steel clicking in place. "Rude, you're with me."

"Where're we going, Sarge?"

"To check on Flight Officer Llewellyn."

Rudipu considered that. "Really?"

"What, you don't want to see his big send-off?"

"Of…course I do, Sergeant."

"Good."

"Sarge?"

"Yeah?"

"What does that mean?"

"You and I are a sniper-scout team," Bolan replied. "We're going to go establish the position of the enemy."

"Oh, shit!"

"You with me, Rude? You can say no and I'll get somebody else, but I'm still thinking you're the best shot in Niner Squad. I'll do the heavy lifting on this one, but every sniper team needs a spotter and a backup shooter."

"Sarge? I don't know if I'm cut out to be a sniper."

"Enlighten me," Bolan said.

"I mean, I love shooting, but I'm with Shelby."

"Who?" Bolan asked.

Rudipu grinned. "I mean, Snake, Sergeant. She and I are both Air Force academy cadets. I want jets."

"I noticed you want Miss von Kwakkenbos, too, Rude. Noticed you noticing someone cut off the top three buttons of her blouse with a machete whenever you thought no one is watching."

Rudipu flushed scarlet, but he salvaged some dignity. "Well, I do like blondes, Sarge."

"Who doesn't?" Bolan liked the cadet's attitude. "So does the enemy, and you do know what they're going to do to her if they catch her?"

Rude looked down unhappily. "Yeah."

"What they'll do to Snake?"

"Yeah."

"What they'll do to you?"

"Sarge!" Rudipu was appalled.

"Rude, this isn't quite the Ninth Circle of Hell, but you can see it from here. There are predators in these woods, four-legged and otherwise. And around here, someone like you is considered a light snack. You understand?"

The diminutive cadet looked down glumly. "Yeah."

"But you have an advantage, Rude. Do you know what that is?"

Rudipu raised his Dragunov. "Precision rifle-fire?"

"That's right, Rude. Precision rifle-fire."

The cadet took a deep breath. "You're right, Sarge. It's time to cowboy up."

"Time to marksman up, Rude." Bolan turned and broke into a light jog. "Try to keep up."

OBUA POINTED AT THE GLADE. "They have buried another one of their dead, Caesar."

"The wounded one?" Segawa asked. "The copilot?"

"That would be my guess." Obua nodded in obeisance to Caesar's consort. "Mama Waldi."

The woman was six feet tall. Though she had the breasts and hips of a fertility goddess, her limbs and waist stretched out like those of a famine victim. Her matted dreadlocks fell to her tailbone. Amulets and fetishes mounded her neck and shoulders. She carried a butcher knife on her belt, and in her hands she carried a *hunga munga.* The African throwing weapon looked like a cross between a hand sickle, a hatchet and a scythe, with a couple of extra knife blades for added effect. It was a weapon that Mama Waldi always sharpened but never cleaned. The edges of the pitted blades gleamed out of the dried gore caking them like quicksilver. Obua had seen Mama Waldi take off a fleeing man's leg just below the knee with one throw. The woman had the flat black eyes of a shark, and she had filed her teeth to points to match. "I want 'em bones, Brother Obua, and all the brethren shall partake of the white bread of his flesh."

Obua licked his lips. It had been some time since he had eaten the long pig done right. The pilot had been crucified and burned with gasoline. It had made his poor flesh a tough and acrid meal. Obua thought about the copilot a day and night in the ground with his juices running. That would be toothsome, meat-falling-off-the-bone fare. "As you say, Mama."

"I want the little one. The girl."

Segawa smiled. "And she shall be delivered to you, Mama."

"Blue-eyed devil woman die in my fire and be our bread."

Obua gave Segawa an alarmed look. The army leader put his hand on Mama Waldi's shoulder. "Not before Brother Obua and the brethren have shown her paradise."

Mama Waldi exposed her pointed teeth. "Then they shall know her flesh in sin and then partake of her flesh as the bread of forgiveness."

"You are wise, Mama." Segawa to where Obua had pointed. Four of the men were busily disinterring the copilot's body with their machetes. "They bury him, brother? Knowing what we would do? Why would they waste the time?"

Obua shrugged. "They are Americans, pale, poor-relation Christians. They are...sentimental."

"Where do you find them now, brother?"

"They make no effort to hide their tracks. They make for the mountains. They make for the Ugandan border."

"Zion," Mama Waldi intoned.

Segawa and Obua spoke in unison. "Holy Zion, the promised land." Obua stared up into the misty mountaintops. "Someone has given them backbone. Given them courage."

"These our mountains. These our forests." Segawa looked at the trail their quarry had left. "They cannot outrun us."

Mama Waldi gazed westward. "I wonder if the white children will turn and fight?"

A huge door-slamming sound answered the witch doctor's question. Birds erupted out of the trees and monkeys screamed as pale orange fire pulsed at the gravesite. The men digging screamed and disappeared in white streamers of burning particulate. Fire crawled up the trees ringing the glade in a burn that moisture would not stop. Only one of the four diggers came out of the smoking curtain. Vusi was barely recognizable as a man. He screamed and flailed at the white phosphorus covering his body in swathes and burning his flesh to the bone.

Segawa drew his *panga.* He took a skipping run forward and wheeled his chopper like a bowler about to pitch a cricket ball. Vusi fell to his knees shrieking and burning. Segawa swung, and Vusi's head flew from his shoulders. His body slumped bonelessly, and his head tumbled down the slope.

Kayizi broke out of the underbrush. He had taken a wide berth around the white phosphorus. He took one glance at Vusi's decapitated corpse and got on with his message. "Caesar! Caesar!"

Segawa took a look at his *panga.* One of Vusi's vertebrae had turned the edge of his weapon. Kayizi was one of the youngest of God's Army. Segawa had turned him into a warrior. Mama Waldi had turned him into a man. Obua had turned him into a tracker. The young man could scent a shadow on a cloudy day. He was one of the most fanatic of the brethren. "Brother Kayizi."

"The trail is clear, Caesar! Ten continue towards the mountain!"

"You count ten, brother?"

"With the pilot and copilot dead? I see all eight cadets, the flight attendant and the commando who leads them! They burn for the Ugandan border!"

Mama Waldi came to stand beside her man. "The American. The commando."

"Yes, Mama."

Mama Waldi's black eyes narrowed. "You would think, a grenade on a body, a playground trick, one we have used ourselves many times."

Segawa nodded. "Yes, Mama. We have."

"Yet we fell for this trick, because we have pulled up their dead before."

Segawa nodded once more. "Yes, Mama."

"The American," Obua scowled. "He reads us, he reads our ways and he has turned to fight."

Mama Waldi ran a disturbingly large tongue over her filed teeth. "Good."

"You buried him with a grenade." Rudipu lowered Bolan's binoculars. "A Willie Pete?"

"I asked him if he wanted to be buried, cremated or left for the enemy. Llewellyn chose all of the above."

"Where was it?"

"He was keeping it under his hat. I kept it under mine, too. I didn't want any arguments. It was his decision."

"I understand, Sarge." The cadet raised Bolan's laser range-finding binoculars once more and watched the milling revolutionaries. They had stopped after the grenade detonation and were having some kind of late-afternoon powwow and boiling a caldron of rice. Rude didn't want to think about what they were having for an entrée. "I count at least thirty. More seem to be arriving. So, should we…?"

"Thin them out a bit?"

"Well, yeah."

"Range me."

"What?"

"Press the button on the bridge of the optics."

Rudipu peered through the binoculars. He pressed the button and caught Bolan's drift. "Twelve-hundred-and-seventy-five meters, Sarge. Sorry."

Bolan peered through the scope of his borrowed Enfield Enforcer rifle. The Enfield design was over a hundred years old. This rifle had been manufactured in the 1970s as a police weapon. Given the combination of rifle and optics, Bolan didn't think he could reliably hit a man-size target much beyond seven hundred meters, and he had yet to fire this particular rifle at all, much less in anger. "Not at this range. Not with this rifle. You?"

The Dragunov was missing its scope. Rudipu shrugged at the ladder of the iron sight. "Well," he said. "It is graduated out to twelve hundred meters."

"I believe the military term for that is cheerfully optimistic," Bolan suggested. "But if you want to give it a try…"

"Well, I have twenty-ten vision, Sarge. But not at this range, and not with this rifle," Rudipu agreed.

"They're making camp. Tomorrow they're going to make a big push to catch up. We start shooting now, and they are going to fan out and try to flank us. We can't win a pitched battle at the moment, and I don't want to play tag with these guys at night, at least not quite yet. We're just going to let them eat."

The cadet made a face. "You don't think they're going to eat their own, do you? I mean, after they've been burned with white phosphorus?

"They can cut around the burned parts."

Rudipu shuddered. Bolan clapped him on the shoulder. "Let's go." They left their grassy knoll and descended into the jungle. The sinking sun disappeared behind the hills and above the canopy, and they were instantly engulfed in shadow. Bolan moved swiftly. The cadet had to scamper to keep up.

"Sarge, how do you know where you're going?"

Bolan knelt and looked at some very fresh tracks. "We're on a game trail, Rude. We're heading west."

"But we're not on Niner Squad's path."

"No, but we're roughly paralleling it. We need to eat and grab some shut-eye, and I don't want to be camping on the path if they get a wild hair to send someone scouting ahead in the night. These guys think they own this jungle, and they're half-right. You and me are going to keep on letting them think that for a little while longer."

Rudipu perked up. "We're going to eat, Sarge?"

"We're rustling up dinner right now."

"Sarge?"

Bolan held up a finger. "Shh..." He unslung his BXP machine gun and began his stalk. The sun seemed to be dropping like a rock. The shadows of the rain forest were turning swiftly into a purple, crepuscular gloom.

A horrific scream tore through the rain forest. The sound seemed to come from inches away. Rudipu just about jumped out of his boots. "Jesus Christ! What the hell was that, Sarge?"

"A leopard."

Genuine fear cracked the cadet's voice. "Sarge, is he hunting us?"

"It's a she, and not at the moment."

Rudipu was clearly relieved. "So...she's just horny or something?"

Bolan's nostrils flared at a noxious, acrid scent wafting through the trees. "No, she just missed dinner." Bolan had been stalking a bushbuck. Fate had provided otherwise. "You smell that, Rude?"

"Gross!" Rude made a gagging noise as the smell hit him. "What is that, Sarge? Skunk?"

"No, Rude." Bolan took out his tactical light and flicked it to the red filter setting. He followed the smell and shone the light into the trees. He stopped and smiled as he found his quarry. "It's our dinner."

Rude looked up and recoiled in horror. "What the fuck is that thing!"

"Language, Rude."

Rudipu raised his rifle defensively. "Sorry, Sarge! But I'm in the jungle here! Help me out!"

In the lurid red glow of Bolan's tactical light something vaguely resembling a cross between a small crocodile and an aardvark that smelled like a septic tank hung by its tail from a low-lying tree branch. It peered myopically into the red glow of Bolan's flashlight. "It's a pangolin, Rude."

"A what?"

"Scaly anteater, of the long-tailed variety." Bolan raised

his weapon. "They have anal scent glands, like skunks. Our leopard friend most likely got a face full, probably two, and retreated. That's in our favor."

Rudipu kept his rifle aimed at the repulsive creature. "So you're saying his ass is out of ammo?"

"Most likely."

"Thank God."

"Hold the light," Bolan said. Rudipu held the light while the soldier aimed. The BXP had no selector switch. A light pull fired one shot and if you went hard on the trigger, it went full-auto. Bolan slowly took up the slack. The BXP made a slight slapping noise, and the pangolin dropped from the tree with most of its head missing.

Bolan slung his submachine gun and drew his South African army knife. "I need you to hold the tail, Rude. Watch out, the scales are razor sharp."

Rudipu took hold of the tail, threw up as Bolan began slicing and promptly cut his thumb. Bolan continued butchering. "Rude, you're going to miss some meals before this is over. You cannot afford to lose one. This is the last time you puke. You read me?"

The cadet wiped his chin. "Yes, Sergeant."

"Pangolins are one of the number one requested bush meats in Africa and Southeast Asia."

"Yes, Sergeant."

"The tail is where they keep their fat. It's the best part."

Rudipu took hold of the back paws and turned his head as Bolan removed the guts. "Yes, Sergeant."

"Delicacy in China, Rude."

"What isn't, Sergeant?"

For a very small man in a very big jungle, Cadet Rudipu had a respectable wellspring of gumption. "Forgive me, Rude. You are a Hindu, I presume?"

"Yes, Sergeant."

"I've served alongside Hindu soldiers, Rude. And I have profound respect for your religion, and you."

Rudipu jerked as Bolan threw a reel of guts into the underbrush. “Thank you, Sergeant.”

“So how strict a vegetarian are you?”

“Well, my mother lets my brother and I eat chicken. She won’t cook it. We mostly eat McNuggets.” The cadet gave Bolan a helpless look. “When I went to academy she told me to eat anything and everything in the dining commons. She wants me to grow big and strong.”

“You ready to eat your first pangolin kebab?”

“Is it a protected species?”

“It’s an armored species,” Bolan replied.

Rudipu gave Bolan a startlingly bold look. “Sarge?”

“Rude.”

“What is your faith?”

“Let’s just say I’m going to eat pangolin on a Friday, Rude. For you, and Niner Squad. You?”

“Karma is a wheel, Sarge.” Rudipu took a long breath and let it out. “I’m going to take a spin for Niner Squad and for you, Sarge. I’m just not letting anyone down on this one.”

“You’ll do, Rude,” Bolan said. “You’ll do.

OBUA LOPED through the morning mist. He and his picked squad of scouts had set out at dawn. Obua maintained a swift pace. His quarry had no skill at covering their tracks nor were they even trying. Obua gave them credit. The white children were marching hard, but Obua and his men could run for days. He did not intend to try to bag the cadets just yet. This day the mission was simply to establish visual contact and keep it while the rest of God’s Army formed and came up. Then the enemy would be flanked, bracketed, placed in a killing box and taken. Obua’s stomach growled. His last two breakfasts and his first experience with white meat had been ruined. The pilot had stunk of gasoline. The copilot had burned to a crisp. Even poor Vusi’s flesh had taken on a very strange tang from the white phosphorus.

Obua considered the flight attendant. He thought of her

every scream and her every pale curve in glowing detail. Saliva oozed beneath his tongue….

Shisho yelled as his leg plunged into a hole in the path. He screamed and clutched the leg that the earth seemed to have swallowed. Obua held up his fist for all scouts to halt. "No one go near him!" Obua took a knee. "Shisho!"

Shisho flopped backward and howled as he dragged his leg out of the muddy, bloody murder hole the prey had dug. Like most of the scouts, Shisho preferred sandals to boots and he often took them off on a run over cut trail. Shisho plucked at the pangolin scales serrating his flesh from ankle to knee and shrieked as it was too painful to pull them out.

"Obua!" Shisho screamed. "Obua!"

Obua ignored Shisho's pain. Instead he tried to push his senses into the forest. Obua's instincts had been jungle honed to a razor's edge.

The forest responded by breaking into an early-morning rain shower. Obua turned his face up into the lashing downpour in acceptance. He had instructed his men to keep an eye out for trip wires. Obua had expected there would be a Claymore, perhaps two. There was nothing to be done about that, except that Obua expected the American would save those to try to stave off the final assault. Obua had also been waiting for the sniper shot that would start the real game.

Instead, the American had killed and eaten a pangolin and made a pungee pit out of its scales. He had done it so cunningly that one of Obua's own scouts had fallen into it and half of his calf had been shredded in the process. The commando had left his calling card. Obua had spent a very instructive part of his Ugandan military training with United States Army Ranger advisers. The Rangers had a word for this. They called it a punk card. The commando had dropped one at Obua's feet.

The American was daring Obua to pick it up.

What had the Americans chanted? *"Hey, ay-ay! Come out and play!"*

"Obua!" Shisho screamed. "Obua!"

Obua crept past his stricken scout and probed the ground

with his *panga*. He found four more pits. Each was about a foot in diameter and two feet deep. Just big enough for a leg to fall through and spaced on the trail so that someone passing would have to fall through at least one.

Obua rose. The path he followed was no longer awkward, desperate footprints of ignorant Western children. That was the draw, and as Obua followed them the white ghost would be there. Every slough of mud was a potential killing zone. Every leaf on the path was now a possible booby trap. This was no longer a hunt. It was war against an enemy engaging in a fighting retreat.

The American was going to fight him every step of the way.

Obua watched as Kayizi pulled finger-long scales from Shisho's leg. "Bind his wounds and leave him. Mama Waldi will tend to him."

Shisho gave Obua an alarmed look. Mama Waldi had a remarkably effective arsenal of native and herbal medicine at her disposal. Obua had seen her bring men back from the brink of death. On the other hand, he had seen her declare injured men unfit and seen them unceremoniously sent to the soup pot.

Every soldier in God's Army was foresworn to never be taken alive.

Shisho's fate was in God's hands, or Mama Waldi's, and in this part of the rain forest they were often one and the same.

"Come." Obua jerked his head toward the mountains before them. "We go."

"DUDE," CADET RUDIPU said, grinning around the last of his morning pangolin. "You took a turd-smelling scaly beast and turned it into a banquet and a booby trap."

Bolan gave Niner Squad's designated marksman a severe look. "Did you just call me dude?"

"No, Sergeant! I mean, yes, Sergeant! Sorry, Sergeant!" Rudipu regained his composure. "So what's on the agenda for today, Sarge?"

Bolan sprinkled some salt on a cube of pangolin rubbed

with its tail fat and chewed meditatively. "I think today we're going to make contact."

"But we already made contact, Sarge. We made contact on them good."

"No, Rude." Bolan gave the cadet's rifle a meaningful look. "I mean today we lay our hands on them. Lieutenant Llewellyn and your breakfast made them careful. That's going to slow them down. Now we give them the thunder and make them justifiably afraid of us."

Rudipu picked up his rifle. "Yes, Sergeant."

"You'll have three jobs. Spot for me, watch my six and keep up. You think you can manage that?"

"Yes, Sergeant."

"We hit them, retreat and hit them again. We do it all day. If they're dumb enough to charge us, I have one or two things in my pack to slow them down, but in the end this fight is going to get ugly."

The cadet nodded. "Always was, Sarge."

Bolan's head snapped up. Rudipu scanned the sky in confusion and suddenly caught the sound. "Sarge, what is that?"

Bolan snagged his phone and hit the Farm preset. Aaron Kurtzman answered. "Striker!"

"Bear! I have rotor noise! Do we have any rescue, evac or mercy flights in my corridor? Military, missionary, UN, anything?"

Bolan could hear Kurtzman furiously checking intel, satellite and signal chatter. "Negative, Striker! No registered flights in your area!"

"Copy that!" Bolan hit the preset for Niner Squad. "Hammer, pick up…." Bolan got the voice mail for the phone he had given his squad leader. Bolan clicked off and called again. Hammer wasn't answering.

Rudipu kept his sights on the enemy. "Sarge?"

Bolan thumbed a text message.

DO NOT MAKE CONTACT WITH CHOPPER

"I swore I wouldn't leave anyone behind," Bolan said.

Rudipu gulped. "Sarge?"

"Try to keep up. If I lose you, just follow Niner Squad's trail." Bolan handed the phone to the cadet. "Worse comes to worst, just keep heading east."

"But, Sarge—"

"Try to keep up, Rude."

Bolan broke into an all-or-nothing run up the mountainside.

6

"Squad!" Cadet "Hammer" Johnson held up his fist. "Hold up!"

"Jesus, we made it…." Cadet Hudjak staggered to a halt beneath the weight of the machine, his pack, and the two other packs that Von Kwakkenbos and Shelby had failed beneath. He dropped to his knees and stared at the vista before him. "Oh, you suck, Hammer."

They had failed to crest the peak by nightfall the day before, and no one had wanted to night march without the sarge. They'd kept a dark camp and huddled together, bundled in all the clothes they had and their dress uniforms. Dinner had been a scant cup of cold rice and a few spoonfuls of peanut butter and jelly. Breakfast had been the same but less. Johnson had set a hellish pace at dawn. They'd hit the summit before noon.

Another valley lay before them.

Another mountain lay on the other side of it.

Niner Squad was crushed at the sight of it.

Cadet Eischen took a knee and threw up.

Cadet King collapsed against a tree trunk. "Yo, Hammer, call him."

Von Kwakkenbos was a wreck.

Cadet Jovich took a look at the woman's feet. She was developing some spectacular blisters. "Blondie's done. Do it."

"No," Eischen rose unsteadily. "Don't."

"No…" Shelby needed a tree to keep standing. "Sarge said not to call until the second day."

Johnson unconsciously looked at Cadet Metard. To his shame, Johnson still saw the senator's son as an authority figure. Metard was bent double but met his eyes. It was too late to look away. "Meat?"

"You're squad leader, Hammer." Metard smiled an exhausted smile. "But if you're taking suggestions, I suggest we stay the course. Sarge knows all about what's between us and Uganda. Nothing unexpected has come up. We're just tired and sore, and that?" Metard looked out across the highlands. "That is damn depressing."

Johnson took a look around the mountaintop and then a long hard look at his first command. He decided he'd be damned if he called up the sarge and complained that there were too many mountains for Niner Squad's liking. "We'll take five. Ace, get the last bag of rice soaking. Donger, weren't you an Eagle Scout?"

King gave Johnson an offended look. "I am an Eagle Scout."

Jovich held up the three-finger salute. "Once an Eagle, always an Eagle."

"So you guys have seen a blister or two in your life." Johnson looked at the flight attendant's feet. "Do we pop those blisters or not?"

"Dunno," King replied. "Do we have moleskin?"

"Ace, we got moleskin?"

Eischen rifled through the jet's medical kit. "We've got an emergency tracheotomy kit, an epinephrine auto-injector." He held up a package and waggled his eyebrows. "A rectal thermometer…" Eischen shook his head. "Can you believe no moleskin?"

King nodded. "We're popping. Get me a needle, a match and the adhesive bandages…oh, and whatever lubricant came with the thermometer."

Johnson looked out over the mountains while King and Jovich went to work on Von Kwakkenbos. Metard and Hudjak joined him. "What do you think?" Hudjak asked.

"We saw the smoke behind us yesterday. Ace swears it was Willie Pete, and I believe him. I think Sarge and Rude are ghosting the bad guys and misbehaving. We were late summitting this peak, but other than that everything is actually going according to plan."

Hudjak sighed at the African expanse before them. "So we just keep marching."

"East for Uganda," Johnson agreed. "Until Sarge tells us different."

"Woo-ooo!" Shelby shot to her feet howling in victory. "Woo-hoo!"

Johnson whirled. "What do you have, Snake! What is it?"

"Look, Hammer!" Shelby pointed north ecstatically. "Look! Look! Look!"

Johnson squinted northward. Then his eyes flew open. "Oh shit! Good eye, Snake! Chopper! Ace! Bring me the binoculars!"

Eischen ran forward with the binoculars that had come with the plane's emergency kit. Johnson scanned the sky. "Jesus, please…" The Huey UH-1 helicopter flew low over the ridgeline and was heading their way. The red-and-white painted chopper sported the badge of the Red Cross on the nose. "Yes! Yes! Yes! It's a rescue chopper!"

Von Kwakkenbos sighed and gave thanks in Afrikaans.

The chopper was far out of visual range, but Hudjak jumped and down hooting and waving his arms like a castrated ape anyway.

"Hey, squad leader!" Eischen grinned and held up the bright orange flare pistol from the kit. "Locked and loaded."

"Do it."

"Hey, Hammer, shouldn't we—" Metard sighed as the bright red star flew skyward on a streamer of white smoke. "Call Sarge first?"

"Right," Johnson grunted. He should have thought of that. "Sorry, I got excited." Johnson dug his phone out of his cargo pocket and started at the screen. He had put the phone on vibrate so it wouldn't ring unexpectedly if they were close to the enemy, and it had also somehow worked itself around the bandanna he had stuffed in the pocket, so that its vibrations had gone unnoticed.

The squad leader found he had two missed calls and one text message. “Awww…shit.”

“What is it?” Shelby asked.

“Sarge’s orders.”

Eischen looked at the smoking flare pistol in his hand as if he suddenly found himself holding a dead rat. “And those are?”

“‘Do not make contact with chopper.’”

“Oh, fuck me,” Eischen snarled.

The helicopter came sweeping along the ridgeline with renewed speed and purpose. Johnson hit his preset. He got one-half of one ring before Bolan came across the line. His voice was strained with exertion and heavy on concern. “Tell me that flare wasn’t you, Hammer.”

Johnson swallowed. “The signal was sent on my order, Sergeant.”

“Do not engage!” Bolan ordered. “Repeat! Do not engage!”

“But, Sarge, they’re coming for us!”

“You think, Hammer?”

Johnson raised the binoculars once more. The helicopter was sweeping in fast. The doors were open. He counted eight men in the back. They all wore commercial jungle camouflage. All of them were armed to the teeth. Two of the men leaned out of the doors on chicken straps. Both men wielded revolving grenade launchers. “Awww…shit. Sarge! I’ve got eight hostiles in the chopper! Heavily armed! Grenade launchers in the doors!”

“Do not engage! Escape and evade! Rude and I are two klicks away and closing!”

“Niner Squad! Scatter by pairs! Scatter! Scatter! Scatter!”

Hudjak threw Von Kwakkenbos over his shoulder and charged into the trees. The rest of the team went buddy system and scrambled for cover. The chopper swept over the peak. The grenade launchers thud-thud-thudded on rapid-fire. Gray gas began spreading across the summit. Eischen had the kit repacked and slung. He had lost his cocky grin. "Christ, Hammer! Tear gas? Again?"

"Difference is we aren't tied up this time." Johnson and Eischen faded into the trees. Ropes cascaded from the chopper above and men in gas masks fast-roped to the peak.

BOLAN FLEW UP the mountainside. He continued to hear the pound of boots behind him and flicked a glance back. Cadet Rudipu ran along in his wake in sprightly fashion. He didn't even appear to be breathing hard. The young man grinned. "I'm captain of the cross-country team at the academy, Sarge! I—"

"Save it for the bad guys, Rude."

Niner Squad's trail was a twisting track of footprints and undergrowth broken up by *pangas*. Bolan increased his speed as he heard the first gunshots. It was an AK in semiauto. Niner Squad was engaged. Bolan ran on for the summit. He grimaced as he saw the tear gas spilling down from the peak towards him. The helicopter came around the summit in a tight orbit. "Rude! I'm going in! Stay out of the gas! Engage the chopper!"

Rudipu raised his Dragunov. He tracked the chopper for half a second and fired. The rifle's recoil rocked him back onto his heels. A black hole appeared in the white paint near the tail. The cadet tracked and began firing in a slow cadence.

Bolan took a deep breath as he reached the summit and went into the gas. The first thing he needed was a gas mask.

He was just going to have to take one.

Bolan drew his pistol and quickly fired three shots. He dropped to one knee and held his breath as his eyes began to burn. A man came running out of the stinging mist at the sound of the shots carrying a silenced submachine gun and wearing fatigues, body armor and a mask. Unmasked and in the gas there was no place for mercy. In a few more moments Bolan would be noneffective. He put a burst from his BXP through the new arrival's legs. The man tripped up and fell hard. Bolan yanked up the man's head by his mask straps and pressed his smoking sound suppressor beneath the man's chin, then squeezed off a single shot. He ripped off the dead man's gas mask, took a moment to spill water from his canteen over his face and blinked. Bolan blew as hard as he could into the mask, then pulled it on. It was a tight fit, and he found himself gasping through the filter but he could breathe and he could see.

Rudipu continued his slow fire of opportunity on the bird above. Bolan heard another AK crack off to his left and followed. He hit the flat of the summit. Shelby, Jovich, Johnson and Eischen lay hog-tied in a squirming pile. Von Kwakkenbos, King and Metard were still unaccounted for. Hudjak was on his hands and knees receiving an epic beating from two men with collapsible batons. Bolan's first burst shattered a gas mask and the face behind it. He took out the second man like he had the first contact. He put a burst into his legs and then a single round up through his hard and soft palate and into the brain. Bolan tore off the mask. Hudjak resisted feebly as Bolan poured water into his eyes. "Huge! Hold your breath!"

Bolan strapped the mask onto the young man's head. Hudjak wept and coughed behind it.

Bolan pressed a fallen weapon into the young giant's hands. "Drag your people back the way you came! Get them out of the gas. Rudipu is back on our six!"

The chopper swept overhead, and its rotor wash actually did Bolan a favor by blasting the gas away in all directions. The Executioner repaid it by burning the rest of his magazine up through the Huey's chin window. The helicopter banked hard west away from the incoming fire.

A spiderweb of cracks magically appeared in the pilot's windscreen and the helicopter lurched crazily. Bolan was going to have to fashion a medal to pin on Rudipu's chest. The soldier reloaded. The chopper wobbled and then dived away down the mountain as the copilot took up the stick. Hudjak laboriously began dragging Shelby off the mountaintop. Bolan went hunting for the rest of his squad. He didn't have to go far.

Von Kwakkenbos lay dropped across a rock. Her eye was

blackened and her lip was split. Her blouse and bra were gone. Her assailant tore at her shorts. The cadets were high-value prizes and needed to be kept relatively unharmed. A flight attendant strangling on tear gas was a perk.

Bolan put a burst through the back of the would-be rapist's head.

The gas was thin here, but Von Kwakkenbos was in bad shape. Bolan bathed her eyes and put the dead man's mask on her. He shoved her rifle into her shuddering hands. "Stay here! Kill anyone who isn't Niner Squad!"

Bolan ran on toward the sound of gunfire. He found himself in a fold of mountainside free of gas and standing over the body of a man with a Type 56 rifle sticking up out of his neck by the bayonet.

"Sarge."

Bolan turned to find Metard sitting against an outcropping. The senator's son had a bloody bullet hole through his left hand. Bolan pulled up his mask as he examined Metard's wounds

"Sarge, I stuck one."

"I saw."

"I told Blondie to run, and I stuck him so no one would hear. But he got off a burst and—"

"You did good." Bolan took Metard's right hand and guided his fingers to the radial artery. "Apply pressure. I'll be right back."

"Miss von Kwakkenbos, she's—"

"She's fine."

Bolan rose. Somewhere nearby King shouted raggedly. "Bring it, asshole! I'll—" The rest of the cadet's defiance broke into a fit of coughing. Vomiting followed. Bolan followed the sound. King was behind a deadfall that was saturated with gas. One of the invaders knelt behind a stump and pulled the pin on another gas grenade.

Bolan put a burst into the back of his legs.

The invader fell against the stump. Bolan stalked forward and stripped him of his mask and kicked away his submachine gun. The grenade bloomed to life in front of the man's face. Bolan vaulted the deadfall. He threw King into a fireman's carry and took him out of the gas. He poured the last of his canteen over King's face, but the cadet had taken lungfuls of concentrated CS and was in bad shape. Bolan put the mask over King's face and put him back in the carry. As he walked, Bolan did math. Johnson had reported eight in the cabin. Two were door gunners. Six had deployed. He'd taken five and Metard had gotten his aggressor.

Rudipu's rifle went into rapid semiautomatic fire.

Bolan looked up as the chopper lurched by overhead. One of the door grenadiers flopped limp in his chicken straps like a rag doll. The UH-1 was a single engine model, and black smoke was pouring out of the exhaust. Bolan caught a glimpse of ragged bullet holes in the turboshaft housing. The Huey's engine shrieked and the bird swung around on its axis as it went into autogyration. The enemy helicopter pirouetted in a slow death spiral into the valley behind them.

Bolan trudged up the mountainside. "Meat, can you walk?"

"Sure, Sarge." Metard was pale, but he staggered after his sergeant.

Bolan stopped at the rock the flight attendant still sat on. "Roos, we're out of here."

Von Kwakkenbos rose and followed, shuddering.

Bolan took his troop up to the top. Tear gas was heavier than air, and most of it had crawled down the mountain or dispersed. Rudipu stood with his rifle at the ready as he watched the helicopter go down behind them. Hudjak had cut his fellow Niner Squad captives free. All were red-eyed, weeping and coughing—they looked like wrecks. Rudipu turned and stared in shock at the topless Von Kwakkenbos. Bolan took off her mask. Rudipu's awe turned to rage as he took in her black eye and split lip. "Sons of bitches!" A stream of Bengali invective followed.

"Rude! Give Miss von Kwakkenbos a hand! Find her a T-shirt!"

Johnson's face was lumped as he stood to attention. "Sergeant! The squad leader regrets to report that he failed to—"

"Hammer, take Donger! Jock-itch! Help me with Meat! Ace! Bring the medical kit! Everyone wash out your eyes and police the area! Collect weapons and gear!"

The weeping and coughing cadets staggered to obey their orders. Bolan went back down the mountainside and collected his one living invader. He'd crawled as far away as he could with his legs shot, but the man had been sucking gas for the past ten minutes. Bolan bound his legs and dragged him to the top by the arms like a human travois and dropped him in the clean air. Rudipu had given Von Kwakkenbos one of his T-shirts. Her head lay upon Rudipu's leg and she wept from more than tear gas.

The cadet gazed coldly upon Niner Squad's surviving nemesis. "You left one alive, Sarge?"

"That's right."

"Was he the one who…?"

"Keep your head, Rude. I got there in time, and no, he's not. This man is an intelligence asset until I say otherwise. Do you understand me, Cadet?"

"Yes, Sergeant."

"Watch him." Bolan then went to Metard. Jovich was applying pressure to his friend's wound. The bullet had punched through his palm at an angle and shattered every metacarpal bone he had except for his thumb. Bolan bound the wound and arranged a sling. He reached into his personal med kit. "You allergic to any medications, Meat?"

"Not that I know of, Sarge."

"This is codeine. It's a broad spectrum antibiotic. I'll give you more and change the dressing at our next camp. You let me know if you start feeling feverish or if your hand starts to feel hot."

Metard's face was pale but he looked steady. "Will do, Sarge."

"It's going to be a while before you put rifle to shoulder." Bolan took his holstered pistol off his belt and the three spare magazines. “Cocked and locked, Meat. Jock-itch, help him get the holster on.”

“Yes, Sarge.”

“And you’re carrying his pack for the moment.”

“Right, Sarge.”

Bolan rose to find Johnson standing before him at rigid attention. His face was lumped and bloody from the beating he had taken. “I am sorry, Sergeant. I let you down. I let everyone down.”

“How so, Squad Leader?”

“I should have kept the squad together. Instead I broke us into fire teams and scattered. The bad guys scooped us up out of the bush like bunnies.”

“The enemy wanted you alive. Scattering forced them to divide their unit. It gave Rude and I the time to get here and allowed me to take them out in ones and twos. If you had stood and fought as a unit, it would have forced their hand and most of Niner Squad would be dead now. You did exactly what you should have done.”

Johnson was clearly moved. “Thank you, Sergeant.”

“Telling Ace to fire the flare?” Bolan leaned in and let his voice drop. “That was not so smart.”

Johnson cast his eyes down. “Yes, Sergeant.”

“I gave you strict communication protocols. I expect you to obey them.”

“Yes, Sergeant.”

“Walk with me.” Bolan took a few steps away from the group. “Hammer, you’re having to learn to lead in the hardest way possible. I understand that. But we cannot afford mistakes. When you fired that flare you put a hole in Meat, got Miss von Kwakkenbos bent over a rock and the entire squad mauled. We took damage today that we simply could not afford.”

Johnson looked close to tears but maintained eye contact. “Yes, Sergeant.”

“The men we fought today wanted you alive. God only knows what the ones following us want, but it isn’t good.

We've seen what they're capable of. These are people who have chosen rape, cannibalism and genocide as a lifestyle. They do it in the name of God, and sooner than you or I care to think about, we are going to have to have a knockdown, drag out fight with these people. But I want to thin their ranks and mess with their minds for as long as possible before that happens. So whenever I'm not around, your orders are very simple. Given a choice, you run rather than fight. Hide rather than engage. This is not a fire mission, Hammer. We are running for our lives. Do you understand?"

"Yes, Sergeant."

"Good."

"Sarge?"

"Yeah?"

"So…I'm still squad leader?"

"Hammer, the situation is I don't have much time to lead you people. I need to be roaming around. So all of our survival will depend on how well Niner Squad works together. I saw something in you seventy-two hours ago. I see it now. You're squad leader until your squad votes you off the island."

"Thank you, Sergeant."

"See to your squad, Squad Leader."

Bolan watched the members of Niner Squad as they geared back up. The cadets who had been captured were bruised and bloodied but otherwise they looked all right. Being tear-gassed twice in seventy-two hours wasn't going to help their wind, but there was nothing to be done about that. Bolan looked westward. Smoke rose out of the trees where the helicopter had crashed through the canopy. He hoped that might keep Segawa occupied for the rest of the day. The soldier glanced on the pile of weapons the squad had gathered. They looked like your standard, silenced, MP-5 submachine guns except that they were free of any markings or serial numbers.

Johnson came back. "Niner Squad, ready to move out."

Bolan nodded and turned his attention to the captive.

Despite the man's swollen face and eyes, Bolan could see that he had a Middle Eastern look about him. His ponytail, mustache and beard were not standard military issue. Bolan used a choice phrase he had learned the last time he was in Tehran.

"Your mother sucks bears in the forest," he said in Farsi.

The would-be kidnapper blinked and almost opened his mouth. Bolan smirked. The man's face froze. Johnson frowned. "What was that?"

"Our friend speaks Farsi," Bolan said.

"He's Iranian?"

"Him and his friends were armed with silenced, sterile HKs and Iran produces HK firearms under license. Their camo is Ugandan military issue and their gas masks are police issue. They didn't have tactical radios. They were communicating with cell phones. That was why I could cut through them so quickly. They never knew they were being hit. I would say they were an ad-hoc team put together and equipped haphazardly. Though I give them credit for the Red Cross helicopter. That was genius."

"So they're Iranian."

The man stared up at Bolan in stone-faced rage.

"Oh, he's Iranian." Bolan just kept on staring at him as he read the man his résumé. "He's Quds Force."

The prisoner gave one damning flinch at the word.

"What's Quds Force?"

"It's a unit of Iran's Army of the Guardians of the Islamic Revolution."

"Revolutionary Guard?"

"Yeah, they report directly to the supreme leader of Iran."

"So they're special forces?"

"Of a kind." Bolan eyed the man lying before him critically. "They're responsible for Revolutionary Guard extraterritorial operations."

"What does that mean?"

"It means he and his men are tasked with exporting the Iranian Islamic Revolution abroad. We knew they were operating in North Africa, now it looks like they've jumped the Sahara."

The man looked around at Niner Squad and gave Bolan a very ugly smile. "You fight beside children."

"Yeah, and my youngest shot down your helicopter." Bolan got right up in the prisoner's face. "How do you like them apples?"

The prisoner clearly didn't.

"So," Johnson said, looking at Bolan uncomfortably. "We interrogate him?"

"He's already told me most of what I want to know, and we don't have the time." Bolan suddenly squatted on his heels. "You know the people following us?"

The Quds operative glared back in silence.

"That's a rhetorical question. I'm not going to torture you, but by the same token I have neither the time nor the wherewithal to carry you with us. I'm leaving you here."

The man could not keep a look of alarm off his face.

"Maybe your people will come and get you. But in the meantime, the people behind us eat humans. They are on their way now. I'm going to ask you a simple question." Bolan took the Browning Hi-Power pistol he had stripped from the man's belt. "You answer truthfully? I leave you with this."

"The Holy Koran forbids suicide except in martyrdom."

"No, I'm going to allow you to die fighting."

The Quds operative looked long and hard upon the pistol and then back at Bolan. "What is your question?"

"Was this a one-shot deal? Or are your people going to try again?"

The man smiled beatifically. "If Allah wills it, my people will take you long before you reach Uganda, unless the savages get you first."

Bolan tossed the pistol ten yards across the glade. "You want it? It's over there."

"Sarge!"

"If he wants his last act on earth to be shooting a member of Niner Squad in the back, he's going to have to crawl for it, and fast. Get your squad moving, Hammer."

"Niner Squad!" Hammer bawled. "Move out!"

Bolan walked over to Rudipu. The cadet stood with his rifle crooked in his arm as if he was going pheasant hunting. He watched Von Kwakkenbos sling her pack. "Rude."

"Sarge?"

"I'm going to take point for a while, blaze some trail. I want you on our six."

"You got it, Sarge."

"You did good yesterday," Bolan told him. "Real good today. How are you holding up?"

"Well, Sarge, so far I ate a pangolin and shot down a helicopter."

"You're coming dangerously close to becoming squad leader, Rude."

"Naw, don't want the job."

"No?"

"Sarge, I'm a pilot, and sniper." Rudipu patted his rifle happily. "We're solo artists."

Bolan nodded. "Niner Squad! Loose file! On me!"

7

Segawa reconnoitered the wreckage from a prudent distance. They had heard the gunfire on the peak and seen the chopper spiral out of the sky. The bird lay on its side with its rotors snapped. An impressive number of holes had been punched in its rotor housing. Obua and Kayizi clambered up the skids and peered inside. "They not Red Cross workers, Caesar."

"Who they be, brother?"

There were two bodies in the cabin. One man hung from his straps in the middle of the cabin like a broken puppet. The man on the opposite door was connected to his straps by little more than goo and had been crushed nearly beyond human recognition. Obua climbed inside and looked in the cockpit. The pilot lay against his side window, missing most of his head. Obua picked up a revolving grenade launcher. Neither he nor any of the brethren had ever fired one, but he was sure he could figure it out quickly. He found a locker filled with gas grenades and smiled. Six of the slots in the case were fragmentation grenades. Kayizi happily began liberating knives, wristwatches and the pilot's handgun. He hooted at a ten thousand euro roll. "No identification, brother."

Obua looked up to find Segawa standing on the side of the fuselage looking down at the carnage. He frowned upon the dead. "They children of Islam."

Obua nodded. The one who still had recognizable features had that look about him.

"Like us, they thought they hunted fat, white sheep, ready

for shearing. Instead the white lion and his cubs have shown their teeth. I believe we will have a battle before us as well, brother, and soon."

"Yes, Caesar." Obua gazed upon the dead man hanging from the fuselage by his straps like a chicken hanging in a shop. Obua was a confirmed cannibal who'd had too many meals missed or spoiled lately.

Segawa read his minion's mind. "Strip the chopper for anything useful and then set the bodies to boiling. Then we march. We push for the top tonight. Once the rest of God's Army assembles, they will bring us our cooked dinner when they come to the encampment."

"Yes, Caesar."

"One question first, brother?"

Obua looked up at his personal savior with some trepidation. Things often became dangerous when the man began asking questions of his brethren rather than giving them orders. "Anything, Caesar."

"Where is the man who flew the bird?"

Obua glanced back at the mostly decapitated pilot. "Missing most of his head, Caesar."

"No, brother, where is the man who crash-landed this bird." Segawa smiled at the empty sideways seat in the cockpit. "Where is the copilot?"

KURTZMAN CLENCHED his fists helplessly on the armrests of his wheelchair. This mission was turning into a worst-case scenario. "Repeat, Striker."

"Repeat, Metard is wounded."

"How bad?"

"Through the hand and shoulder. He's stabilized and walking, but he could go septic at any time."

Kurtzman closed his eyes. He didn't have enough fingers and toes to count the times Mack Bolan had been given up for lost. But Kurtzman had never once given up. Never had he ceased searching for an angle for him. This was the first time Bolan had ever had eight teenagers and a flight attendant under his wing and the only words Kurtzman was authorized to utter was no. Aaron Kurtzman took Bolan's every request like a body blow.

"Repeat," Bolan said. "Requesting immediate extraction."

"Negative, Striker."

"Repeat, requesting immediate reinforcement."

"Negative, Striker."

"Repeat, requesting immediate resupply."

Kurtzman hung his head. "Striker?"

"Yeah?"

"I have been told to inform you that a Skyhook extraction is in the planning stages on Metard. There could be a resupply drop on the other end of it."

Kurtzman knew he was only the messenger, but he flinched at the arctic cold in Bolan's voice. "Tell me you are kidding me, Bear."

"You know how it works. We can only do it once or twice at best. Not ten times." Kurtzman felt sick as he transmitted the rest of Bolan's options. "Failing that, I am told to inform you that you are authorized to escape and evade. The cadets killed or captured are a nightmare. You captured and tortured by these people is a worst-case scenario."

The line was silent for a long time.

"Negative on the latter. Prepare Skyhook and advise."

"Striker, I—"

"Will inform. Striker out."

BOLAN LOWERED the sat phone. In his War Everlasting he had fought every kind of human evil imaginable. He had beaten evils that had threatened the entire planet with radioactive fire and tailored biologicals that would kill by the millions. He had beaten evil that had sought to topple entire nations and the balance of power with the pull of a single trigger or the stab of a knife. Bolan stared up into the African night. This was no international emergency. No weapons of mass destruction loomed over entire populations. No global conspiracy raised its head before Hercules like a Hydra. Bolan stood beneath the jungle canopy of a corner of Africa most humans had never heard of much less cared about. His mission objective consisted of rescuing eight prep-school students and a flight attendant. Bolan had demanded their obeisance and Niner Squad had delivered. He was the angry, Old Testament God of their universe. He had turned them into a unit. Bolan hadn't promised them anything even close to salvation, but the children of Flight 499 believed Bolan would deliver them onto the Promised Land. They believed in him. In the past seventy-two hours, this had become one of the most personally important mission of Bolan's career.

Bolan was beginning to get the feeling that this was the battle he might lose.

Bolan ran every possible angle for the hundredth time. Without extraction or reinforcement, there just weren't many angles left to run. He was on foot with eight teenagers and a flight attendant. He already had wounded and the simple fact was that the Congo stood between him and Ugandan plateau.

The Executioner began to do the terrible math of mission triage.

He could extract Metard via Skyhook. Rudipu just might run out of this place, but he was in love and he would never abandon Von Kwakkenbos to the ministrations of Caesar Segawa and his legion. Bolan considered what little he knew of Julius Caesar Segawa. Bolan thought he might be able to fight off the Iranians, but they would still be waiting across the Ugandan border and would be planning a much larger interception force across it. Segawa and his horde would never stop. Bolan thought of all the threats he had faced, all the terrors he had met and conquered, all the international situations that could never be spoken of that he had solved.

And here on this day cannibal Ugandan hillbillies wore the face of Nemesis.

Bolan knew deep in his heart neither he nor Niner Squad would ever reach the Ugandan border alive. There had to be another way.

Bolan walked back to camp. They had marched until the

very last shaft of light had disappeared from the forest. Niner Squad huddled around the low-banked fire as what was left of the pangolin simmered. It would be eaten with the last sack of rice. "Meat! You have a ticket home!"

Metard looked up from his plastic cup of pangolin broth and blinked. "What?"

"It's called Fulton STARS extraction. A C-130 will drop an extraction pack. It will consist of a cable, a balloon and a strobe. We will harness you up and deploy the balloon and the strobe. The C-130 will return. A catch device on the nose of the plane will harvest the balloon and pull you up. The team in the back will reel in the cable and pull you in. We should expect it within the next twenty-four to forty-eight."

The campsite went silent with this bit of news. Metard put a hand on the butt of the pistol that Bolan had given him. "Anyone who tries to tie a balloon to my ass gets two in the face."

"Nice answer, Meat, but you're going to slow us down. Take the get-out-of-jail-free card and go."

Eischen grinned and raised his hand. "I'll take his slot, Sarge!"

"Your carefree, breezy will to abandon your squad mates is noted, Ace."

"No, I mean, if he doesn't want it 'n' stuff…"

"No." Metard looked to Von Kwakkenbos. "Give it to Blondie."

Rudipu scowled. "They won't come for her, jack-wagon."

"Yeah, but they won't know it's her until they pull her in."

Shelby cocked her head. "Jesus, Meat. It's like you have a soul and everything after all."

"Whatever. Sarge? Give her my slot."

"No." All eyes turned on the South African flight attendant. She hugged her knees and looked into the fire steadily. "They will shoot at the plane. When it drops off the kit, and again when it comes for extraction."

"They're Air Force Search and Rescue," Bolan said. "It's what they get paid for."

Von Kwakkenbos sniffled. "And won't it give away the squad's position?"

Bolan nodded. "There is that." Niner Squad looked up at him defiantly. "You're determined, then?"

Niner Squad rose to its feet as a unit. Johnson looked around his squad and all of them nodded. "We are, Sarge."

Niner Squad had made up its mind. So had Bolan. "Then we head north."

Niner Squad's iron resolve changed to mild alarm. "Sarge?" Eischen asked. "Uganda is east."

"Forget Uganda, Ace, we'll never make it."

King consulted his mental map. "Sarge, there's nothing north of here but Sudan."

"And the Central African Republic," Bolan corrected.

"The CAR?" Eischen consulted his mental map. "Oh…fuck me."

Shelby wrinkled her nose. "Sarge, isn't Uganda closer?"

"Oh, it's close, Snake. Tantalizingly close. Problem is, we are walking uphill, out of the Congo, to get to the Ugandan plateau. It's mountain-valley, mountain-valley after mountain-valley. You include the vertical parts of the real estate, and Uganda starts looking real far away and the Iranians will be there waiting for us."

"Sarge." Eischen was not happy. "Last I heard, they eat people in the CAR."

"Last I saw they were eating people here, Ace."

"Oh…right."

"So it's the CAR then, Sarge?" Jovich asked.

"I haven't made up my mind on a destination, just a strategy. First off we double back. It's the last thing the enemy will suspect, and everything will be downhill. On top of that, that's the direction all the rivers drain."

Johnson saw it. "Nice!"

"That's right, Hammer. First river we hit we buy, borrow or steal a boat. We do some distance and ditch it. Then we march for the next river and do it again. We can't outrun Segawa and his bunch on land, but on the water, with a lead, one or two leapfrogs and we should be able to lose him."

Johnson and Hudjak fist-bumped. "Yes!"

"Don't start celebrating just yet, Cadets."

"Sorry, Sarge."

"You're marching tonight."

Shelby sighed. "Back up the mountain?"

Bolan took out his binoculars. "Everyone take a look back. Through the break in the canopy. Directly the way we came."

Niner Squad passed the optics around. A slow wave of discontentment moved through them as they made out the tiny, flickering orange firefly lights of campfires on the mountaintop. Johnson handed the glasses back. "What if we hit 'em, Sarge? What if we hit 'em tonight?"

"I thought about that, Hammer. They're up there right now eating an Iranian marinated in tear gas and thinking tomorrow is the day they run us down. I know you all want some payback, but my first goal is to get you all out alive. Meat has already taken one for the team. We cannot afford more wounded. I am going to march you up the mountain, past their camp and then you are going to follow the trail straight back down to the valley floor and turn hard north. I have satellite intel that there is a navigable river fifty klicks north of the valley. If I'm not back, you just march north until you hit the river and then start taking it west and follow the plan. Let the Bear guide you."

Rudipu leaned on his rifle. "You want me along, Sarge?"

"I do, Rude, but we've established you can run with these guys and you can shoot. If I'm not there, you are the one who is going to make the difference. Shoot, then fade back. Shoot, and then fade back again. You outrange each and every one of our pursuers. Make them pay for every foot of ground."

"I understand, Sarge."

"Knew you would, Rude."

Bolan looked to the squad leader. "Hammer, I want everyone ready to move in an hour. We took two flashlights from the wreck. Put on the red filters. Do not turn them on unless given permission. We are three blind micing it up the mountain. It's going to take most of the night, but my people will be GPSing us a route. Everyone finish your food. Hammer, divvy up the squad in two halves. First half gets a twenty-minute power nap, and then the second. Then we ruck up and go."

Johnson nodded. "Ready in an hour, Sarge."

"Good, I'm going up the trail a bit on watch. Kill the fire and set your sentries."

Bolan walked out of camp as Jovich and King killed the fire and Johnson assigned naps. Bolan hiked a few hundred yards up the mountain. He found a nice spot between a crown of tombstone-sized rocks and unlimbered his rifle. He was proud of the squad. Despite Segawa's terror and the mauling by the Iranians, they were showing teamwork, selflessness and remarkable esprit de corps. It would all come down to making the river and getting a boat. Metard's wound was still clean. No one was sick yet. Bolan lifted his binoculars and looked towards the peak. Hopefully he could get lucky just one more time.

Bolan watched the enemy's camp. A single, 500-pound GBU-22 bomb would settle Segawa's hash and that of his little army quite nicely. Unfortunately, Bolan didn't have a laser designator and there were no United States Air Force A-10 Thunderbolts flying over the Democratic Republic of the Congo this morning. On top of that, the morning fog shrouding the peak had put the kibosh on the morning sniping. Bolan couldn't get a good read on the enemy numbers but he was betting it had increased to over fifty, and he had the feeling more would be arriving with the sun. The fog had allowed Niner Squad to reach the top of the mountain and start its descent unseen two klicks north. Bolan's job was to entice God's Army to go the opposite way.

The camp slowly came to life. God's Army didn't seem to be in any hurry. The guerrillas rose in ones and twos and yawned, urinated and performed whatever passed for morning ablutions in this corner of the disputed Congo. Several went over to the cook pot and pulled out some very suspicious looking pieces of food. God's Army was so self-assured it bordered on the lackadaisical. So much so that it took fifteen minutes from the first man rising to someone noticing that the sentries from the last watch were missing.

Consternation broke out in camp.

Bolan's thumb rested on his remote detonator. His supply of high explosives was extremely limited, and it nearly broke his heart to use some of it nonlethally, but the name of the game today was to break contact with Segawa and his little legion, hopefully once and for all. Bolan clicked the button and on the western side of the mountain about an ounce of C-4 made a "thump" sound. The soldier pulled the pin on his last CS gas grenade and lobbed it through the fog into the middle of camp. More shouts of alarm broke out as the morning fog took on a very unpleasant aspect for everyone's optical and respiratory membranes.

With any luck God's Army would think it was being attacked from the eastern face of the ridgeline.

Bolan hit his detonator again, and another ounce of C-4 popped downslope. He took his last white phosphorus grenade and lobbed it into the haze of gas and mist. Shrieks and screams broke out as smoke and fire turned the morning miasma lethal. Orders roared out in conflicting English, Swahili and Ganda. A few local recruits bawled out in French. Bolan raised his silenced submachine gun and peered through the red-dot sight as the camp spasmed away westward from the irritant gas and burning metal.

There was one other strategy at play.

A single subsonic hollowpoint bullet through Julius Caesar Segawa's skull might end this ugly farce at the source. Bolan had read what little Kurtzman had been able to text him on God's Army. Segawa would never stop. However, with Segawa's head split open to the sky, there was a chance his second in command, Obua, might just be smart enough to pick up his marbles, assume the leadership while he was at it, and go home.

The white phosphorus and tear gas served their purpose. Men began firing down the western slope at everything and nothing. Others scooped up their few belongings and charged westward to get out of the gas and superheated smoke. Bolan scanned for Segawa, but the peak had literally turned into the fog of war. Four men broke out and charged down the path Niner Squad had taken the day before, firing from the hip as they went.

Bolan hit his detonator and one of his two Claymore mines

slammed over the sound of the cacophony in camp and shredded the intrepid four. The blast seemed to focus Segawa's men like a lens. They streamed down the mountain in direct attack, oblivious to any more traps that might await them. Bolan had to give them credit. They were true believers. He wrinkled his nose as the gas started to creep towards his hiding place. They were true believers who were going to spend the day going down the mountain the wrong way and then spend the night going back up. Bolan checked the increasingly bare shelves of his candy store of unpleasant surprises. He thought he might have one or two he could spare for God's Army's hike as they tracked Niner Squad's trail back up the mountain.

Bolan rose and began his run along the ridgeline. The fog would be clearing soon, and he wanted to link up with Niner Squad by noon.

OBUA PICKED UP the grenade. God's Army was in disarray. Two men were dead from the white phosphorus. Most of the recruits were charging down the mountainside hacking, choking and firing their weapons as they went. Obua and his picked men had stayed by their leader. Obua dropped the still hot cylindrical casing and blew on his fingers. "Caesar."

Segawa was in a fine rage. "What, brother!"

"This grenade was thrown, not launched."

Segawa's rage instantly abated. His reddened eyes flicked to the tree line along the ridge. "And the other?"

Obua glanced over to the smoldering, blackened spot on the ground where the white phosphorus had bloomed. "I cannot tell, Caesar."

"Heard two detonations down the mountain, then the mine."

"True."

"Where's Brother Kayizi?"

"Down the mountain."

"Call him."

Obua took out his cell phone and punched in Kayizi's

preset number. Obua put the tracker on speakerphone. Kayizi coughed on the other end of the line. "Yes, brother!"

"Hold up the men."

Obua could hear Kayizi bellowing down the trail for the men to halt. "We are halted."

"The white children's trail?"

"A child could follow it, brother. It continues down the mountain."

"Take two men, go slowly. Go careful. Find where the explosions happened. Tell me what you see."

"Yes, brother!"

Segawa stroked his beard in thought. "The White Lion, he plays his games with us, brother."

"So I believe, Caesar."

"He is a deep one, this White Lion. I think perhaps he might have spots."

Obua smiled. Lions had long symbolized might in Africa. Leopards were the symbol of cunning. "Perhaps, Caesar."

"No matter what he does, he cannot hide his children's trail."

"No, Caesar."

"So he sends us headlong down the mountain after them. While he is here. That is no way a leopard protects its cubs," Segawa mused. "And like a leopard with cubs, no matter what he does, he must return to them."

Obua nodded. "And so?"

Segawa looked westward and lifted his chin in disdain. "This trail does not interest me. Call Brother Kayizi. Tell him when he has finished his task to continue down the mountain. If he makes no contact, come back on the run. Meantime, brother, find our missing sentries. We wait for the fog to lift and the men to recover." Segawa turned north and gazed along the ridge. The mist was beginning to shred and turn to steam as the sun rose. "Then find me this leopard's trail."

SERGEANT MAJOR Heydari Pakzad marched steadily through the jungle. He had, Allah be praised, emerged from the crash in rather remarkable shape. His left eye was swollen shut and he had taped his broken ring and little finger to the middle as a splint. He was on foot in the Congo, but his situation could be far worse. The extraction team had packed emergency rations and a large medical kit in case they had found the cadets in starving, injured or sickened condition. He had one of the grenade launchers and a bandolier of munitions as well as his issued weapon. He had ample bribe money, a compass and a map, and back in Uganda he rose every morning at dawn and went on a ten-kilometer run. He felt confident. Pakzad's real problem was communication.

As an operative whose primary training had been in signals, communication and intelligence gathering, it was particularly galling to be in a position where he couldn't get a signal. The radio in the helicopter was in ruins. The team had decided not to risk tactical radios. The Americans might not be able to project any force into the northeast Congo, but there was no doubt their satellites would be listening very intently. It was Pakzad's own idea to issue cell phones. The ones issued were sterile, acquired locally, same day, and not of the latest manufacture.

Pakzad needed to get out of the valley.

He would let the Americans and the savages following them head west. He had route marched the past twenty-four hours along the valley floor and headed north for the river. Pakzad checked his watch. It was 2:00 p.m. He wanted to hit the river by four. Once there he would rest and—

The sergeant major went sprawling as the predator dropped on him from out of the trees. Pakzad ate the loam of the forest floor as his breath was blasted out of his body. He rolled over, clawing for his weapon. His stunned body and the packs he carried made him a few heartbeats too slow. He gasped as an unfriendly knee pinned him in place at the sternum. He found the cold muzzle of a sound suppressor hovering over his face.

Bolan spoke very quietly. "Hi."

Pakzad considered an appropriate response. "Hello."

A voice spoke from back in the trees. "Sarge?"

"Bring up the squad." Bolan looked down on his captive. "Where're you headed?"

Pakzad saw little reason to lie or conceal anything. Being reasonable was both his best weapon and survival strategy for the time being. "I cannot seem to get any reception in this locality—Sergeant, is it?"

"It's a problem around here," Bolan agreed. "Where're you headed?"

"I thought I would let you and the native contingent contend with each other on your trek eastward. I would head north. Once out of the valley I would try to reestablish contact with my people, and perhaps come upon a village or even a town. Unlike you, no one hunts for me. If my people could not extract me, I would arrange river passage to the provincial capital. There I would book a flight out of Bangoka International Airport."

"Not a bad plan."

"But I see you have doubled back."

Bolan let the obviousness of the statement stand for itself.

"Bold," Pakzad said. "But what do you hope to achieve?"

Niner Squad came down the path. "Look!" Hudjak grinned. "Sarge caught another Quds guy."

Pakzad started in surprise as the young giant casually identified him.

"Wish he'd caught another pangolin," Eischen grumbled. It had been a good eighteen hours since Niner Squad had eaten anything.

"Donger," Bolan ordered. "Search him."

King yanked off Pakzad's two packs and then started from the feet up. He removed the prisoner's boot knife and pistol, and handed off his grenade launcher and submachine gun. King took a wad of euros from a plastic bag and rifled through it. "Ten thousand." He tugged an elastic money belt out from under Pakzad's waistband. The cadet looked up as he opened the Velcro. "Gold, Sarge!"

Bolan looked at the twenty gleaming coins. "Islamic dinars.

They trade big across North and Central Africa. Particularly in places where people wipe themselves with paper money."

King took Pakzad's watch, compass and cell phones and moved on to the packs. "Medical kit, some zip restraints, a pair of handcuffs." He moved to the next bag. "This one's heavy..." King's jaw dropped. "Food, Sarge!"

Niner Squad unconsciously crowded closer.

King tore open the box and scowled at the writing on the individual ration packs. *"Sauté de lapin? Agneau aux flageolets?"*

Bolan had eaten French rations before. Their freeze-dried stuff was just about inedible. Their individual reheatable rations were about as good as field rations got. "That's sauté of rabbit. The other is a kind of mutton stew."

Von Kwakkenbos stopped just short of drooling. "Mmm... mutton."

King looked at Bolan pleadingly. "Can we, Sarge?"

"He brought it for you, Donger." Bolan smiled over his suppressor at Pakzad. "Didn't you?"

"Yes, in case the cadets were malnourished."

Bolan glanced at the cans of food. He admired the man's carrying ability. "The problem with French ration packs is that they're heavy."

"Be a lot lighter soon, Sarge!" Eischen sang out.

"Right. Ace, Snake, mess detail." Eischen began cutting open ration packs. Shelby sorted while Bolan read out the menu for the next twenty-four hours. "For anyone who cares, rations one to seven will have pork, eight to twelve won't. Each meal will have two canned entrées. Eat one now, cold, and save the fuel tabs. You can have the next one hot tonight. Save the powdered soup, crackers and spread for breakfast tomorrow."

"What about the candy and stuff, Sarge?" Shelby asked.

"Hard candy and gum is up to each individual, Snake. Save the chocolate and the energy bar. That might be all there is for dinner tomorrow."

Snake looked over at the captive with mild hostility.

"What about him?"

"What about him?" Bolan replied.

"Well, do we feed him?"

"How about we feed him to Segawa?" Eischen suggested. "His guys must be hungry, too."

"Don't know." Bolan raised an eyebrow at the prisoner. "What about you?"

"You need me."

Metard's voice was as cold as the grave. "Mister, I need you like I need a hole in the hand. I say we kill him."

Bolan eyed Metard. "You down for that job, Meat?"

"Oh, yeah, and I'll make him eat one of the pork entrées first. Terrorist son of a bitch."

Pakzad regarded the wounded cadet with mild alarm.

Johnson frowned. "Meat's half-right. He's a terrorist. They're suicide guys, or at least expendable. His people won't bargain or trade for him."

"No, they will not," Pakzad admitted. "But yours will bargain or trade for you."

Jovich stabbed an offended finger at Pakzad. "The United States doesn't negotiate with terrorists!"

"Of course not. Not openly, or directly." Pakzad smiled. "But indirectly, and through third and even fourth parties. I assure you pleasing accommodations have been reached with the West before. Often with far less at stake. Surrender to me and I will see that you are removed to a safe place and humanely treated."

Jovich snapped open his bayonet. "Sarge, if you don't cap his ass, I—"

"Jock-itch! Bolan snapped. "When does the squad fix bayonets?"

Jovich snapped to attention. "When ordered to or under direct attack, Sergeant!"

"Keep that in mind."

"Consider this," Pakzad soothed. "You are in Equatorial Africa. I am fluent in French, Swahili and Arabic, and have engaged in business dealings with the locals both here and across several of the neighboring borders."

Bolan kept his poker face. Pakzad had him there. A communications asset like Pakzad would increase their chances of survival a hundredfold. "So far, we have two votes for death. What does the rest of the squad say?"

Niner Squad stared at the prisoner in a terrible new light. They were the jury. Bolan was the Executioner.

King spoke first. "Sarge, we're Americans. We don't rape or murder prisoners." The cadet looked back toward the mountain. "And we don't eat them, either. That's the difference between us and him, and us and them."

"Donger's right," Shelby said. "We can't just murder him, and we can't leave him operating behind us."

"We're in the Congo," Rudipu said. "He speaks French."

"I don't trust him," Eischen said. "But I think we might need him."

Johnson nodded. "I agree. He came to capture us. Now we own his ass. I say we make him work for it."

Hudjak squatted beside the Quds operative. "You know, for a little guy, he's a hell of a pack mule. I wouldn't mind him humping Blondie's and Meat's packs for a while."

Bolan looked at Jovich. "And?"

"I didn't mean it. I mean, I did, but—"

"Blondie?"

"Let him live."

"Meat? You seem to have a real hard-on for this guy."

"He's an asset until you say otherwise, Sarge."

Bolan rose. "Listen up. I've fought Quds Forces before. They're picked for their loyalty to the Islamic Revolution and the supreme leader, but they are not your wide-eyed for Allah martyrdom suicide types. They infiltrate and arrange these activities for others. What I am telling you is that Niner Squad will not have a kamikaze in its midst, but a serpent."

Pakzad looked pained by the comparison.

Bolan didn't care. "So here are the rules, friend. If you want to live, you're going to have to eat. If you want to eat, you're going to become a genuine asset to this squad."

"I underst—"

"You do not speak unless spoken to. The first time you do, I will kick your teeth down your throat. The second time, I will blow your brains out. You will obey every order given to you by any member of Niner Squad. The minute you fail you will be killed and your body left for Segawa and his people. Do you understand?"

"I understand. May I ask the status of my people?"

"All of them were killed in the battle, except one. He was wounded through the legs. I left him a pistol and a bottle of water. Your people found him or Segawa's did."

"I see."

"Anything else?"

"Yes, I—"

"No? Good. Donger, cuff him. Hands in front. Snake, feed him one of the tins from packs eight to twelve. Everyone chow down. We're walking in ten minutes. Huge, Jock-itch, when the prisoner is done eating ruck him up with Blondie's and Meat's packs."

Bolan snagged himself a tin of Chicken and Greens Parisienne and a packet of indeterminate fruit drink. He spiked his canteen with about a third of the packet to add some electrolytes and sugar. The cadets observed and quickly followed suit with their commandeered canteens and water bottles. Bolan cracked his tin and slopped cold chicken and slimy greens. He watched Metard open his tin by holding it between his feet so he could pull the tab with one hand.

Bolan shoved his bite of food to one side of his mouth. "You know what your problem is, Meat?"

Metard lifted his chin manfully. "The cadet regrets to report that he has many! To which is the sergeant referring?"

Bolan kept the smile off his face. "You're a goldbricker, Meat."

Metard looked at the tin of French mystery meat between his feet and then at his sling. "I am?"

"Yeah, your 'I'm a just a little brown duck with a broken wing' routine is starting to chap my hide. I'm giving you a job."

"Sarge?"

"Prisoner detail."

Metard looked over at Pakzad. "Thank you, Sarge."

"The prisoner will walk in the middle of the file. You will walk behind him maintaining at least a three-yard distance at all times. Pistol drawn, round in the chamber, hammer down. Safety off."

Metard brightened to his task. "Prisoner protocols, Sarge?"

"If he does anything funky—" Bolan crushed his empty French ration tin in his fist "—shoot him."

“So what should we call him?” Shelby asked.

Niner Squad filed through the forest. Metard frowned. His arm was killing him, but he would rather die than ask the sarge for painkillers before they were issued to him. “What do you mean?” the injured cadet asked.

“I mean we all have names, Meat, and he’s part of the squad now.”

“How about the Prince of Persia?” Eischen called out.

“Little long.”

King grinned back at the captive. “We could call him Poppy, or Popper for short.”

“Popper,” Von Kwakkenbos smiled sunnily. “I like it.”

Metard grinned malevolently. “How about Xerxes.”

Pakzad reddened. The Islamic Republic of Iran considered the film *300* and its portrayal of the Persian fourth King of Kings a national affront.

“Ayatollah?” Hudjak suggested.

“Of Rock ’n’ Rollah?” Rudipu countered.

“I vote Qudsy-poo,” Shelby said.

Pakzad snarled something under his breath.

Bolan seemed to materialize out of nowhere. “What did I say about talking?”

Pakzad flinched. It bothered him a great deal that he found himself afraid of the big American. “You said I should not speak unless spoken too. I believe I was being directly insulted by the entire squad, and I spoke in Farsi.”

"Forgive me. We haven't been formally introduced." Bolan pointed his BXP in Pakzad's face. "Name and rank."

Pakzad flinched. "Pakzad, Heydari." He salvaged some pride and lifted his chin in the face of the weapon. "Sergeant Major."

"Paki!" Eischen grinned. "Even better."

"Niner Squad!" Bolan snapped. The squad snapped to attention. "This man is not a member of the squad, nor is he a pet. He is a prisoner. You will treat him with respect. If you find yourself in a situation where he needs disrespecting, you should have shot him already. Clear?"

"Clear, Sarge," Niner Squad acknowledged in unison.

"Until we all part ways, you will refer to him as Mr. Pakzad," Bolan lowered his weapon out of Pakzad's face. "Can you live with that?"

"It will be sufficient, until we part ways." Pakzad's eyes narrowed as he peered eastward over Bolan's shoulder. "Though that may be in the afterlife."

Bolan looked back. A break in the canopy showed the mountain they had left behind. The sun was just beginning to dip in the sky and shone upon the mountain face. The Executioner frowned as he suddenly caught a glint on the mountainside and then another. He brought up his binoculars and his gaze narrowed at what he saw.

Johnson appeared at Bolan's side. "What is it, Sarge?"

Bolan dialed the magnification on his optics to maximum. God's Army was stopping just short of plunging down the mountainside in pursuit. He handed Johnson the binoculars. The squad leader's jaw dropped. "Awww...shit."

"They didn't fall for it. I had hoped to buy us at least a day, maybe two. If we march hard they won't overtake us before sundown, but if we don't find a river and boat really quick, tomorrow there's going to be a fight."

Pakzad held up his manacled hands. "I strongly suggest you give me a gun."

Metard put his pistol against the back of Pakzad's head. "No one spoke to you, Mr. Pakzad."

Pakzad rolled his eyes and looked at Bolan plaintively. The big American nodded. Pakzad drew himself up. "Those men are not my allies, nor an ally of my nation. If what you say is true and one of my men was still alive when you left, then I hope he died fighting, for otherwise what will have befallen would be unspeakable. They are savages, and I do not wish to be taken by these savages handcuffed and ready for their cook pot. They track you. That means they are tracking me. We are now in this together. I give you my word I will fight beside your squad with all of my ability."

Bolan took back his binoculars and took another long look at the men streaming down the mountain. "Meat, cut him loose."

"Sarge!" Metard was appalled. "I—"

"I'm going to need every man tomorrow, Meat. Donger, give him whatever he wants from the gear we took from his outfit."

Metard unhappily uncuffed the prisoner. Pakzad rubbed his wrists and retrieved a silenced submachine gun, twelve magazines, his pistol and a short, heavy bush knife as asked. Pakzad checked his loads and slung his MP-5 over his shoulder. "Am I to gather that conversational standards have been relaxed?"

"To a degree," Bolan said. "And I think you know what that degree is."

"I understand. No inciting unrest or mutiny. However, I have a request."

"Spit it out."

"Should we survive, and reach one of the major river ways, I request that you give me a cell phone with a battery in it and a reasonable sum of the money you have taken from me. I will arrange transportation for myself to the capital, and we shall part ways amicably."

"Take a walk for a minute."

Pakzad walked a discreet distance away. The squad formed on Bolan. "Anyone got anything to say?"

Metard spoke for everyone. "Sarge, you really trust this guy?"

"I trust him for exactly as long as he needs us to survive. I want two pairs of eyes on him at all times. At night when half the squad is on watch, I want at least one sentry watching him. If I'm killed, kill him immediately. Meat's standing orders still apply. If he does anything funky, kill him. Don't wait on orders from me. Meantime he's a sergeant major in the Iranian Quds Force, and he'll probably account for a fair number of the enemy tomorrow if it comes to it."

Niner Squad nodded solemnly.

"Mr. Pakzad!" Bolan called.

Pakzad walked back into sight. "Yes?"

"You looked like you had a destination in mind this morning. A river?"

"Yes, not a major one, but there should be villages somewhere along it, and where there are river villages in the Congo, there are canoes."

"Can we make it by nightfall?"

Pakzad looked around the squad. It was pretty clear he thought he could do it, but wasn't sure about them. "Possibly. If we push hard."

"Good enough, take point. Keep heading where you were going."

"Very well."

"Hammer, push hard. I want that river by sunset. Rude and I will catch up."

"You'll have that river, Sarge. I guarantee it."

"Don't waste your breath talking about it, Hammer. Do distance. Do it now."

"Squad, on Mr. Pakzad!" Johnson shouted. "Move out!"

Rudipu sidled up next to Bolan. "I'm your prom date again, Sarge?"

"Rude, some might describe you as irrepressible."

"Well, Ace is the squad comedian, Sarge, but I've found if you're a sniper spotter long enough you develop a certain gallows sense of humor."

"In ninety-six hours?"

"How long is ninety-six hours in sniper years, Sarge?"

Bolan measured his spotter. Cadet Gupti Rudipu was a little man in a very big rain forest with nothing between him and personal Armageddon except a rifle as big as he was. Though that wasn't quite true. Rudipu had an ace in his back pocket. It was quickly becoming clear that he had a heart bigger than the mountain they had just left behind. "A lifetime, Rude."

Rudipu nodded. "Figured."

"Rude?"

"Sarge?"

"I look forward to saluting you."

The cadet blushed like he'd just looked down Von Kwakkenbos's T-shirt. "Sarge, I was born in the Silicon Valley. Three blocks from the Apple Computer campus. I'm a U.S. citizen. After some stick and rudder time in the Air Force, I have inclinations about running for President of the United States."

"I've worked for worse," Bolan said. "Let's go bag breakfast."

Rudipu perked up. "Pangolin?"

Bolan hadn't stopped Niner Squad just to establish Sergeant Major Pakzad's status. He'd noticed tracks. The soldier knelt and took a closer look at the small, fifty-cent-piece-size footprints at the side of the trail. The creatures that made them were supporting themselves with only three of their toes. Bolan could hear the trickle of a creek nearby. "Bush cutters."

"Is that some kind of little deer?"

"Greater Cane Rat."

Rude's eyes went wide. "Sarge, you can't ever tell my mom."

"MMMM..." Cadet Shelby's eyes just about rolled out of her head as she tore into her spit-roasted morning meal. "What is it?"

Rudipu rolled his eyes prosaically in return. "Just close your eyes and pretend it's chicken."

"Better than chicken," King proclaimed.

Bolan bit into a leg. The French said that hunger was the

best sauce. Thirteen-pound cane rats rubbed inside and out with French ration pack salt, pepper and olive oil mixed with a healthy dose of hunger and hiking through the Congo was making for about the best breakfast anyone in Niner Squad had ever eaten.

Perfectly seared cane rat turned to ashes in Bolan's mouth as his least favorite app rapidly began peeping into life on his phone. He had jumped into the Congo with a packet of eight paired, golf-ball-size motion sensors. He had deployed three of them already. He'd gotten occasional peeps as something had broken the infrared beams between them. Suddenly he was getting rapid chime after chime. Either a herd of forest elephants was passing along Niner Squad's trail or God's Army was at two miles and closing. Bolan rose.

Johnson jumped to his feet. "Is this it?"

"It's a prelude." Bolan calculated klicks and topography. "Segawa and his main force couldn't have gotten here this quickly. He's a guerrilla fighter, so he keeps his people spread out, but he's calling them all onto him now. I'm betting that some element of God's Army was already here in the valley. They're onto us and want the glory of bringing their leader the prize, or at least pinning us down until he gets here."

"So what do we do?"

Bolan's phone kept chiming. He figured the bad guys' numbers were at twenty plus and rising.

"Douse the fire?" King asked. "Break camp?"

"Finish your food, Donger. That goes for all of you."

Niner Squad stopped short of tossing their heads and slurping their cane rat down their gullets like crocodiles. Pakzad watched Bolan with interest as he ate. The members of Niner Squad devoured their food in record time. "Sarge?" Hammer asked.

"Douse the fire. Break camp and do it clean. Then take the squad down the trail another fifty yards and double back. Huge, put yourself behind those rocks. Blondie, assist him with the belts like I showed you. Everyone else by your pairs. I want a cross fire on this glade with Huge hosing down the middle. Stay concealed. If it comes to it, this is a pop-up operation. Wait for my signal."

"Sarge?" Eischen asked.

"Ace?"

"So we're shooting them?"

Jovich shook his head. "Jesus Christ, Ace!"

There wasn't any of the usual mirth in Eischen's face. Bolan held up his hand to quiet the muttering. "What's on your mind, Ace?"

"How many times?"

"How many times, what?"

"How many times do you shoot a man?"

The glade grew quiet.

"You shoot him until he falls down, Ace. Then you shoot the next one until he falls down. You keep shooting until they're all down or we are."

Eischen regarded his Type 56 rifle soberly. "Copy that, Sarge."

Pakzad unslung his silenced submachine gun. "And myself?"

"We can't afford casualties. I want to see if these guys can see reason. Failing that, we put them in a killing box."

"I see. So you on one side of the campsite and I on the other."

"Exactly. Follow my lead."

"Agreed."

Bolan nodded at Johnson. "Hammer?"

"Sarge?"

"You're still here. Given the terrain, I'm giving these guys ten-minute miles. You got five and counting."

"Niner Squad! Break camp! Move out!"

By silent agreement Bolan and Pakzad walked north thirty yards and then doubled back. Bolan broke west and Pakzad east in a circle around the camp. They both stopped in the underbrush. If the glade was a watch face, they were at two and ten o'clock. Bolan nodded, and they both squatted on their heels and disappeared in the undergrowth. Niner Squad disappeared up the trail. Bolan winced as he listened to the click and clack of Hudjak and Von Kwakkenbos setting up their machine-gun nest. The rest of the squad managed a modicum of quiet as they took their positions.

It took three minutes rather than five.

A God's Army scout silently came into the glade through the shrubbery a few yards left of Niner Squad's trail. He wore his sandals around his neck and stared very long and hard at the dirt-quenched campfire and the mass of footprints gouging the loam all around the glade. He eyed the trail that headed northward out of it. The scout rose and beckoned backward with his hand. Heavily armed, barefoot men began filling the glade in frightening silence. They had been running hard but the sound of their breath barely broke the quiet of the forest, which was one big hush at the emergence of so many predators.

A man with braided hair and a similarly accessorized beard walked into the glade and peered about. Bolan raised his weapon, aware that the rest of the squad followed his lead as the man walked to the northern edge of the clearing and examined Niner Squad's trail heading into the bush. The platoon leader turned and looked long at the smothered fire. He kicked the dirt and smiled at the embers that rose like sparks. He snuffed at the burned cane-rat juices that wafted up and nodded at his men. "Ten minutes' rest. Brother Bertram, make some coffee. We take them within the hour."

Bertram squatted by the fire and began blowing it back into life and pulled a pan from his pack. "Yes, Brother Todd."

Bolan counted twenty-five. He watched as the two squads smoked cigarettes and snacked. Brother Todd pulled a smoked hand from beneath his camo and began gnawing at the base of the thumb.

The Executioner stepped out of the shrubbery. "Gentlemen."

God's Army was remarkably disciplined. As Bolan had suspected, they had teased armed villagers out of their huts before slaughtering them. Brother Todd lowered his snack and smiled. "You the white boy."

"White man," Bolan corrected.

Todd shrugged. "Caesar calls you the White Lion."

"My respects to mighty Caesar."

"What you want?"

"I want you to go away."

Pakzad stepped out of the shrubbery on cue. "So does the supreme leader of Iran."

Brother Todd's eye flicked to the edge of the glade. "Where the children?"

"Marching."

Brother Todd's braids danced as he shook his head. "Can no outrun us."

"I know." Bolan's open money belt lay looped over his ankle. He kicked it out at Brother Todd's feet. "Twenty-five thousand U.S. dollars."

Brother Todd sneered. "Caesar cares nothing for money."

"Does Todd?"

Brother Todd eyed the money belt in the dirt before him. Part of him did. "Split between twenty-five, it's no so much."

A thousand greenbacks was a small fortune in this part of the Congo, but Pakzad took up his end seamlessly. "I have euros."

The men held their weapons and looked back and forth between Brother Todd and the two foreigners. They had been in the jungle for a long time. For some the idea of some R and R in a real town or city with pockets full of cash was tempting.

Brother Todd ran a tongue across his lips. "And so?"

"So drink your coffee," Bolan said. "Have lunch. Follow us in a leisurely fashion. When Caesar catches up tell him we reached the river and the trail stopped."

"Hard." Todd tugged his braided beard ruefully. "Hard to play Caesar for the fool."

"Hard to die here with nothing to show for it."

Brother Todd sighed. "Put it to my men?"

"Make it fast."

Brother Todd turned and spoke to his crew Swahili. Bolan knew only a few words in Swahili. *Kill* was one of them. God's Army suddenly raised its weapons.

"Now!" Bolan roared.

He heard the pop of Metard's pistol first. AK rifle-fire cracked on semiauto as Niner Squad sought targets, and then all was stuttering thunder as Hudjak laid in with the RPD. Bolan began shooting the second he'd given the order. He had mastered the trigger pull on the BXP to produce reliable double taps. Bolan aimed and fired at a burst per heartbeat. The range was point-blank. The members of God's Army jerked and fell as Niner Squad's surprise cross fire reaped them like wheat. Bertram the coffee maker threw up his hands where he knelt by the campfire, screaming his surrender.

Pakzad burned him down with five bullets in the back.

Bertram fell face-first into the embers and seemed to be beyond caring. Twenty-five men had crouched or stood in the glade. Within five seconds all lay on the forest floor.

"Niner Squad! Sound off!"

"Snake! Meat! Huge!—" The squad sang out.

"Form up!" Johnson led the squad out of hiding while Bolan and Pakzad covered the glade. "Niner Squad presented and accounted for, Sarge. No casualties or wounded."

"Caesar's on his way. Strip them. Ammo, gear, anything of use."

The squad stared around the glade at the dead and dying men.

"Sarge?" Shelby asked.

Bolan knew what the question was but allowed it. "Snake?"

"Some of them are still alive."

"We don't have the time or the meds. Their own people will be here directly. We leave them where they lay."

"We render unto Caesar the things which are Caesar's—" Johnson paraphrased the Bible as he pulled an AK out of a dead man's clutching hand "—and unto the sarge the things that are the sarge's. Niner Squad, loot and scoot!"

Bolan nodded to himself. Johnson was coming along nicely.

“Sarge!” Johnson’s voice rose in urgency. “Sarge!”

“Rude, eyes on our six!”

“Copy that, Sarge!” Bolan loped back to the front of the column. Niner Squad had made contact. They stood in a clearing with their weapons leveled. What appeared to be a prune with eyes, nose and mouth stared back in trepidation. The old man wore an old jean jacket with no shirt, cargo shorts and what looked like locally manufactured sandals. The man’s rail-thin body resembled beef jerky. He held up his hands. In his left he had a string of a dozen rope squirrels. In the other he held a single barrel shotgun. Around his neck he wore a Roman Catholic cross, and an old French Lebel revolver hung by shoelaces from its lanyard ring.

“I don’t think he’s God’s Army, Sarge.” Johnson looked at the man curiously over the front sight of his rifle. “But I thought you said there weren’t any villages nearby.”

Bolan eyed the antique revolver and noted the squirrels had all been taken with clean head shots. The primitive shotgun was leopard insurance. “He’s a hunter in the bush-meat trade. That means the river is close. He’ll have a boat. He hunts for a day or two, mostly small game, and then sells the meat and skins downriver. Everyone lower your weapons.”

Niner Squad lowered their muzzles. Their guest lowered his shotgun and his squirrels. *“Parlez-vous anglais?”* Bolan asked.

The hunter gave a not-so-much shrug. *“Vous? Français?”*

Bolan shrugged back. “Mr. Pakzad, translate for me.”

“As you wish.”

Pakzad translated nearly as fast as the two men spoke.

Bolan introduced himself. “I’m the sergeant.”

“I am Franco.”

“We’re lost.”

Franco smiled to reveal mostly missing teeth. “Oh?”

“We’re hungry, too. How much for the squirrels?” Bolan asked.

“What do you have?”

“Do you take dollars?”

“I prefer euros.”

Bolan reached into his pocket and pulled out a coin. “How about gold?”

Franco regarded the gleaming, Islamic dinar between Bolan’s thumb and forefinger. “Everyone likes gold.” Caution and cupidity fought across his face. “You must really like squirrel.”

“I prefer cane rat. Pangolin is even better.”

Pakzad stumbled a little on cane rat, but Franco nodded at Bolan’s taste in bush meat. He seemed hypnotized by the coin. “I am tracking a herd of red river hogs. Do you eat pork?”

“There’s no time.”

Franco’s eyes flicked between Bolan and Pakzad. “Oh?”

“Julius Caesar Segawa is coming this way.”

Franco’s eyes bugged out of his wrinkled face as he began babbling something in the local dialect.

Pakzad rolled his eyes. “Franco is alarmed to the point he has lost his French.”

Franco shook his head and got it back. “Caesar never comes this far west, not since the soldiers from Kisangani beat him a year ago.” He gave Bolan a hopeful look. “They were trained by Americans.”

“Caesar comes for us, Franco.” Bolan gestured at the ground. “Now that your tracks are mingled with ours, I am very sorry to say he’s coming for you, too.”

Franco threw a miserable glance at his feet. Most were

missing nails, and the left was missing the ring toe. "This is not good."

"You have a boat. Will it hold all of us?"

"Yes, I mean, no. I—" Franco stared ruefully at his feet once more. "Once I throw out the skins I have taken."

Bolan reached into his pocket and came out with jingling dinars. "One for dinner and a boat ride out of here. Another for your services as a guide for as long as it takes us to get to safety. A third when we part company." The Islamic dinar pinged off Bolan's thumbnail. Franco caught it. It had been some time since Bolan had seen someone bite a gold coin to test its value. Franco had to work it pretty far back to get a molar on it.

"Maybe some euros if you're cooking is any good."

Franco grinned from ear to ear as he took the coin out of his mouth. "Deal."

CAESAR SEGAWA's fist clenched in rage. He stared at the river where the trail ended abruptly. All Brother Todd had to do was to make contact, pin the quarry or just slow it. Instead he had gotten himself and his men slaughtered. The scene they had come upon in the glade had been appalling even to Segawa. He opened the pouch around his neck and dipped in the tip of his French paratrooper knife. He came up with a heavy chef's pinch worth of methamphetamine and snorted it.

God was testing him.

He knew the answer to his question, but he asked anyway. "The white children? They were here?"

Obua knelt by the riverbank and read the area like a crime-scene investigator. The footprints of the cadets were as clear as scripture. So were the combat boots of the American, now known as the White Lion, and the Iranian. Obua peered intently at the track of a pair of tire-tread sandals. "A local boy has helped them, Caesar."

"Local boy should know better, brother," Segawa snarled.

Obua looked at the telltale gouge in the riverbank where a

large canoe had been beached. "One local boy, with a great big canoe. I say he's a poacher."

Mama Waldi appeared from her walk downstream. She held up a sodden and expertly cleaned monkey carcass. "Brother Obua be right. Poacher-man throw away his harvest. Take on the white children as his cargo. Bet he been paid with the child of Islam's gold."

"Black man of Africa—" Segawa dipped his knife into his pouch and gave the other nostril a dose "—serving the Iranians and the colonizers. Special place in hell for him." He slapped his stomach. "Special place in our cook pots!"

God's Army cheered. The cheers died down as they looked downriver. God's Army had often acted as a riverine force. However in the attempt to run down the cadets they had failed to bring any canoes with them. Segawa's fists paled as he clenched them. "My heart and mind are fire. Mama, where is wisdom?"

"Brother Obua wants him a Boer whore. You and me want the little Latina between us. We all want to see the white children take the sacrament and kill themselves some UN men."

Segawa felt his senses clarify as the methamphetamines ripped through his mucous membranes. He knew his woman had an idea. "And, so?"

"And so they upon the waters. We have no boats. They head west." Mama Waldi smiled her shark tooth smile. "Call the Serb, Caesar."

Segawa was pleased. "Obua?"

"Yes, Caesar?" the man answered.

"Make the call."

Nzoro township, DRC

"CHILDREN?" THE SERB, otherwise known as Nenad, leaned out over his balcony and watched the Nzoro River flow beneath him. He scoffed into his cell phone in French. "Are you smoking hemp again?"

Obua was silently offended for a moment on the other end of the line. He had given up hemp when he had joined Segawa's ministry and God's Army. "I thought you liked children, Captain."

It was the Nenad's turn to be silent. He rubbed the salt-and-pepper stubble blanketing his head and scratched at the matching stubble covering his face. The dark rings under his sunken eyes were so dark and deep that he looked like he had been kicked in the face while looking through a pair of binoculars. That and his jaundiced, burned yellow complexion were the result of several Equatorial African diseases having tried and failed to kill him. He was a big man, but Africa had eaten every spare ounce of flesh off his frame. Despite his cadaverous appearance, he radiated power. In more ways than one everything that had tried to kill him, and many had tried and failed, had made him stronger.

He chain-lit another unfiltered Gauloises cigarette and flicked the butt into the dark water below. "These are American children you are taking about? Just walking about in the bush?"

"A plane load of military cadets, going to South Africa. Iranians shot them down. The Iranians tried to claim them near the border but were killed. Caesar thought you might find this of interest."

"It is intriguing, Obua, as an anecdote, but what are American children walking through the forest to me?"

"Long has it been since you have been Mama Waldi's guest for dinner."

Nenad unconsciously licked his liverish lips. The Serb had conducted a number of direct transactions with Julius Caesar Segawa and had developed a taste for Mama Waldi's menu. And Obua was right about one thing.

The Serb liked young people.

"Now you say they are on foot? Near the border? That is a great deal of exposure for a man in my position."

"No, Captain. They are in a boat. They are heading west."

"On what river?"

"One of many with no name, but it will lead them to the Nzoro River. The Nzoro leads to the Uele, and Uele will lead them to freedom."

Nenad smiled for the first time during the conversation. "And the Nzoro leads to Nzoro town, and that lies through me."

"So Caesar says."

"Caesar is wise. How many?"

"Eight cadets, one flight attendant. Be warned they are armed and are fighters. It looks like an American Special Forces man leads them like Moses. Also with them walks the one surviving Iranian, and a local hunter. We think he is guiding them."

"That far east?" Nzoro was a hub for the bush-meat and poaching trade, and he was heavily involved in it. There weren't many local hunters left. Most of the poachers in the Congo these days were gangs of men who sprayed their quarry to death on full-auto. Some of them were so inept they were reduced to putting land mines on established game trails. They saw real hunters as competition and frequently killed them. "That might be Franco Zakuani. He ranges pretty far."

"Is this Franco reasonable?"

Nenad considered what he knew about the wizened old hunter. It was said he had led river safaris when there were still French around. These days he specialized in live small game, particularly rare birds and animals sought by Asian collectors. Any bush meat he shot he generally ate, and any excess he sold to the villages along the rivers. Years ago Nenad had moved a few specimens for Franco, but as the Serb's empire in Nzoro had grown, Franco's trade had become too small to care about. From what he remembered Franco was deeply religious, deeply tribal, scrupulously honest and had been in the forest by himself for far too long. "Not in any way that will be helpful to us."

"I see."

"Tell me, what are Caesar's wishes in this matter?"

"Caesar thinks you might know of some likely lads. He thinks you might be able to locate a boat or two."

On a face like the Serb's a smirk was a terrible thing. "I might know a boy or two who can handle themselves." He looked down at the pair of French speedboats docked beneath his balcony. "And the river is full of boats."

"So Caesar has hoped."

"And what might Caesar see as the disposition of spoils?"

"The sons of Islam carried money in case they had to pay for the children. Caesar cares nothing for mammon. But if it pleases the captain, then ten thousand euros are yours, success or failure."

Nenad watched the Nzoro River pass beneath him. For a man like him it was a decent chunk of change, but chicken feed and they both knew it. "What else?"

"The little Latina is Caesar's and Mama Waldi's. The flight attendant is mine."

"And?"

"The Commando had dollars. At least twenty-five thousand. It is yours if we take him."

The Serb's bruised eyes went reptilian. "And?"

"And Caesar wants the white children for his Ghost Squad. They are not for sale or ransom. They will become part of God's Army."

"And?"

"The black or the Paki. You may have either."

Nenad's bruised eyes opened in interest. "What does that mean?"

The Serb's phone chimed as he was texted a photo. He scowled at the picture of John Henry Johnson tied, kneeling and glaring up into the camera phone that had taken his picture by the fallen plane. He touched the icon for the next text and the photo of Cadet Gupti Rudipu weeping, bound and cowering beneath Flight 499's wing filled his display. Nenad whispered to himself in Serbian. *"Oh my..."*

Obua did not speak Serbian but his voice smiled across the line. "We have a deal, then?"

The Serb marched back into his study and connected the USB cable between his phone and his PC. "We do." He downloaded the photo and began enhancing it. "I will call you when my team is on the water."

"Very good."

"Tell Caesar to go to the place of our last rendezvous."

"We already march there, Captain."

"Very good. We will feast after our victory. Tell Mama I crave her liver and onions."

"Mama Waldi will be pleased to hear, and pleased to provide."

"Give Caesar and Mama my thanks." Nenad touched his phone off. His life had been spent putting himself into positions that allowed him to make a profit and at the same time satisfy his appetites. It was a delicate balance. He decided he needed to hedge his bets. He touched a received call from earlier in the day. The phone rang and a feminine, sunny, English by way of Uganda voice answered. "Hadaf Tea and Coffee Company, Uganda. How may I assist you?"

The Serb's uncharacteristically gleaming eyes never left Cadet Rudipu's image. "I am returning Mr. Rhage's call."

FRANCO COULD COOK. His rope squirrel and wild onion fricassee left both Bolan's barbecue and French reheatable ration packs in the dust. Twelve squirrels barely fed twelve humans, but along with balls of *fufu* flour moistened in the gravy Niner Squad ate its fill. The squad had all learned the phrase *merci beaucoup,* and Franco grinned happily as he ladled out gravy and dumpling seconds to any cadet who applied.

Franco's canoe was the traditional, hollowed-out trunk of a tree. As a well-to-do hunter by Congolese standards, he had a small outboard motor and a few aluminum hoops that supported an awning. It could just fit Niner Squad and ride perilous inches above the water line. Franco had remarked through Pakzad that even the laziest, summer sunstroked crocodile could snatch a cadet. Franco cackled like a rooster with a herniated testicle at the response among the cadets.

Bolan licked his fingers clean. "Mr. Pakzad, please tell Franco he's a good cook, and thank him."

Pakzad translated. Franco grinned from ear to ear. Pakzad sighed. "Franco says if you give him one more coin, he will have both enough money and material to get new gold teeth in Nzoro."

"Tell him if he gets us to Nzoro alive he can have gold, ivory, porcelain, whatever he wants. It's on me."

Franco gave Bolan a very steady look as he spoke. Pakzad nodded as he translated. "Franco says you are a good man. He says he enjoys feeding you and your children, but it has been hard to be a toothless hunter, sucking *fufu* and pot sauce while everyone else around the fire enjoys the meat. You are kind to an old man."

"Tell Franco if we are both alive a year from now, I look forward to tearing into water-buffalo tongues in cassava leaves with him at the *nganda* of his choice."

Nganda restaurants were a Congolese intermediary between bars and restaurants. Traditionally unmarried women owned them. Franco stifled a sob and wrung his hands as he bobbed his head in turtlelike fashion and spoke fervently to Bolan. Pakzad sighed once more. "Franco is praising your ancestors in Swahili."

"Praise upon the ancestors of Franco."

Pakzad took a confidential step or two towards Bolan. "Allow me to prevail upon you."

"Prevail away."

"Allow me to call my people. They may not be able to provide direct extraction, but they could put a large amount of money in the right places in the towns before us. The right magistrate or local commander could be prevailed upon to bring us in," Pakzad said.

"You don't think the CIA could do the same but better?"

"I would imagine so, nevertheless you seem quite reluctant."

"I'm reluctant to contact anyone or stick my head up anywhere until..." Bolan raised his head. Something throbbed below the sound of the river and the wildlife of the day. Pakzad caught it and looked toward the clouds in the west. "Thunder?"

Bolan looked at Franco. The hunter had already heard it and was blinking and bobbing his head like a man talking on the phone. "No, drums."

The members of Niner Squad craned their heads and peered upward as they strained to hear.

Franco nodded as the sound stopped. A few moments later a drum that was much closer picked up the sound. Even to Bolan's untrained ear the message was being repeated. Bolan nodded to Franco and Pakzad took up the conversation.

"What's the range?"

"Five miles, if it is a village-size one. One to two if it is a handheld drum."

"I was pretty sure there weren't any villages nearby."

"Even in times of peace, and I am an old man who has never known them, villages move. Slashing and burning new land. Following the fish. Following the hunting. The rivers, particularly the small ones, often change course. Now there has been so much fighting, so many refugees. Who knows where or when you will wander upon a camp."

"What do the drums say?"

"The White Devil is upon the water."

Bolan refrained from sighing. It just kept getting worse.

Pakzad frowned. "He says the interesting thing is that the message is traveling from both east to west and west to east."

Johnson looked heavenward for strength. "Great, they got us coming and going."

"Translate that," Bolan said.

Pakzad did and Franco shook his head. Pakzad narrowed his eyes at what he heard. "Franco says the two messages are different. There are two White Devils upon the water. The one moving west can only be you, but the one moving east he knows."

"Ask him if he happens to have a drum with him."

Franco's wrinkled brows rose at the question. "Only city dwellers and the latest generation go out into the world without a drum."

"The Albino Spider Unto Whom All Things Come?" Kurtzman made an amused noise. "Hell of a handle."

"That's how we know there are two white devils on the water. Drum talk isn't like Morse code. You can't print out someone's name like John Smith. The drumbeats approximate human speech, so it all has to be said in mutually accepted words. You need a descriptor and something that distinguishes it to make an identifier. If the drummer knows what a bear is, you would be 'the Bear Who Plans War' or 'the Bear with a Brain the Size of a Casaba Melon' and everyone would know which bear was being talked about."

"Well, thank you."

"Everyone of any note in a locality has a drum name. Franco is the only local I've met, so I don't have one. Segawa is Ugandan, so he doesn't speak the local drum talk. He must have had one of his local recruits send the message. Tone and context is everything in drum talk. He wants the locals to drum whenever a white devil is spotted so he can keep tabs on us."

"Sounds like a pretty loose tail."

"Enough to tell him which fork in the river we might have taken, or if we're back on land and marching."

Kurtzman mentally chastised himself. Drum talk was something he should have factored in to the equation. "And the other message?"

"The other message came eastward, out of Nzoro. It's a general warning. The white devil by the name of Albino Spider Unto Whom All Things Come is upon the waters. To the locals it means watch your ass. Franco says everyone in this neck of the woods calls our albino spider the Serb. That enough for you to give me a name?"

"It is, but you're not going to like it."

"Who?"

"Captain Dragan Milutin Nenad, Yugoslav People's Army Ground Forces, retained his captainship in the reconstituted Army of Serbia and Montenegro." Kurtzman sighed unhappily. "Transferred to the Bosnian Serb army. White Wolves special unit, adviser to the Bosnian Serb militias. Implicated in the Srebrenica massacre and for war crimes during the siege of Kosovo."

Those words told Bolan just about everything he didn't want to hear.

Many Serb veterans had fled after the final partition of Yugoslavia to avoid being prosecuted for war crimes. So many had joined the French Foreign Legion under the national origin "Slav' to get new identities that the legion had been forced to change some of their recruiting policies. Others had gone on to use their skills in some of the very darkest and war-torn corners of the Earth. President Mobuto of Zaire had hired large numbers of Serbian vets to prop up his regime. Mobutu was long gone, and Zaire had become the Democratic Republic of the Congo, but the violence that stretched across Equatorial Africa from coast to coast had rolled right along to the present day.

To this day Interpol received a steady trickle of rumors of individuals of Eastern European origin misbehaving in the region.

"What do we know about him?"

"As you can imagine, not much. He operates in a region that's considered a backwater even in the Congo. Some reports by UN Peacekeeping Forces indicate his specialty seems to be the recirculation of small arms. The DRC army and UN Peacekeeping Forces regularly sweep villages and towns throughout the Orientale Province for caches of small arms. It seems they often sell them to Nenad. Some of the peacekeepers have gotten into trouble for selling their own issue ordnance and declaring it lost in combat.

"Nenad pays in hard cash and immediately turns the weapons around and sells them back to the militias and rebels. Reports from the capital lead me to believe that he's started selling weapons downriver to the ever-growing Congolese drug gangs."

"He's made himself a middleman."

"It looks like he gets paid back in drugs from the cities. He then exports them back down the river ways into the hinterlands east and north. In return he gets diamonds, poached ivory and animals from Garamba National Park that the locals can't easily dispose of."

"Through his European connections," Bolan surmised.

"It's also rumored that with all the displaced people and refugees, he's gone into trafficking humans and organs. The arrangement seems to bring in profits that stagger what he initially pays for rusty AKs, slipshod surplus submachine guns and RPG-7 rocket-propelled grenade launchers in dubious condition."

"The Albino Spider Unto Whom All Things Come," Bolan said. "It's appropriate. He sits in the center of his web, and the rivers of the Congo bring him profit in every direction."

"He's a real, live heart of darkness situation," Kurtzman agreed.

Bolan had a feeling that whatever Captain Nenad had done in Bosnia—things that the United Nations War Crimes Tribunal desperately wish to try him for—were very likely to have paled in comparison to the atrocities he had seen, personally explored, and if Nenad was on speaking terms with Julius Caesar Segawa, tasted, in over a decade in the Congo.

"How's the squad holding up?" Kurtzman asked.

"Well, Franco's been a godsend. Niner Squad has been able to put their feet up and rest for the last twenty-four hours. Franco cut fishing poles and put them to trawling to keep them occupied. We had fricasseed squirrel yesterday, and the local equivalent of fish tacos and stewed mystery fruit for breakfast. It's remarkable that no one's gotten sick yet."

Pakzad flashed his eyes at Bolan, who looked to where he glanced. Metard sat against the prow of the boat. He was sweating like everyone else in the river camp, but he was white as a sheet rather than flushed. "Bear, I'll get back to you."

Bolan ended the call and strode across camp. "Meat?"

"Sarge?"

"You look like crap. Show me your hand."

Metard brought up a shaky hand to unwrap his wound, but Bolan pushed it aside and did it himself. His nose twitched at the faint smell coming out of the wrapping he had changed the previous night. Several members of Niner Squad gasped. The remains of Metard's fingers were swollen, leaking sausages. His palm was scarlet. Red lines had begun to radiate toward his wrist.

"Meat." Bolan grimaced. "Why didn't you tell me about this?"

"I didn't know it was this bad. I didn't want to hold up the squad. I figured if we could just get to a town or..." Metard bit his lip in pain and shame.

There was no time for recriminations. Bolan rose and whipped out his phone. "Bear, I need immediate extraction for Metard."

"Striker, you are too far away from the Ugandan border for Fulton STAR Extraction. They stood down. I'm going to need—"

"Copy that." Bolan rose and looked to Franco. "I need your largest butchering knife, and I need it shaving sharp."

Niner Squad paled as a unit. Franco started crying as Pakzad translated, but he nodded and went back to his boat. Metal began ringing on stone.

"Donger, I need the remaining morphine, the surgical needle and thread, and—hell, just bring everything."

"Yes, Sergeant."

"Jock-itch, stoke the fire. Boil me some water."

"Yes, Sergeant."

Bolan looked at the ragged, internally rotting remains of Metard's left hand. Things went septic in the tropics in the blink of an eye. The soldier blamed himself, but there would be time for personal recriminations later. He concentrated on the task at hand. Bolan had plugged more bloody holes and wound craters than he could count. This, on the other hand, was surgery, and his patient had a long distance to travel before he ever saw a medevac chopper.

"Sarge?" Cadet Shelby looked as green as the jungle foliage around her.

"Yeah?"

"I sew really well. I mean, if you want me to…I can."

Bolan leaned in close. "Snake, I'm cutting off Meat's hand. There's going to be more blood than you've ever seen. Then I'm going to pull the skin from the top of his forearm over the stump with pliers. We're doing this because infection has set in, and reinfection is most likely going to kill him. I'm not saying I'm any good at this at all, but how clean and tight you sew him up will go a long way in determining whether he lives or dies."

"I'm volunteering, Sarge."

Bolan nodded. "When the time comes, I'll hold the fabric for you."

Shelby gulped. "Thanks, Sarge."

Franco approached holding a curved boning knife with a gleaming new edge. Metard shuddered at the sight.

Bolan took the knife. "Rude, take your rifle and keep an eye on the river east. Ace, you keep an eye west."

Pakzad spread his tarp out without being told. Metard shook like milk as he was laid back on it. King began laying out everything they had left in the medical kit. Bolan put the knife in the pot of boiling water Jovich brought to him.

"Huge, hold his legs. Jock-itch, hold his other arm. Hammer, I need you to keep the infected arm immobile. Put your thumb on the femoral artery when I tell you. Blondie?"

Von Kwakkenbos blinked in surprise.

"Put his head in your lap. Smile so he won't be afraid."

The members of Niner Squad arranged themselves around Metard. Bolan washed his hands with a sterile wipe and took the knife out of the pot.

"Meat, you know what I'm going to do?"

"Yeah, Sarge." Metard just about bit through his lower lip. "Do it."

"Donger, shoot him up." Bolan nodded at Johnson, and the squad leader jammed his thumb into Metard's inner arm. Cadet King gave Metard the last auto-injector in the thigh. Metard visibly sagged.

Bolan tied the limb off. "How do you feel, Meat?'

Metard sighed at the syrupy warm haze floating through his veins. "As good as I'm going to for a long time, Sarge."

"You know something, Meat? For a punk kid you're coming along just fine."

Metard gave Bolan a dopey smile. "Sarge?"

"Yeah?"

"Do me a favor?"

"What?" Bolan asked.

"My hand…"

"What about it?"

Metard sighed again. "Don't leave it anywhere that Caesar shithead can find it and eat it."

"You got it. I'm going to start on three. Ready?"

Metard's eyes rolled. "Ready, Sarge."

"One." Bolan cut hard, fast and deep. Metard gasped in shock. His eyes focused into terrible clarity. The human wrist bone was a major joint, and one cut wasn't going to do it. Bolan worked the joint as fast as he could without being sloppy. Despite 20 mgs of morphine and Von Kwakkenbos's soft embrace, Metard screamed like a young man having his hand cut off with a butcher knife in the Congo.

BOLAN DRANK the cold dregs of the coffee Franco had made. He sagged against the bole of a tree. The tree sat on a little rise and gave him a view of the camp and a bit of river in both directions. He clicked on his night-vision goggles for a few precious seconds of battery life and looked through his binoculars. Nothing moved on the Nzoro River except the river itself. Bolan clicked the off goggles and forced himself to take five. He wasn't at the end of his rope, but like he'd told Rudipu, you could see it from here. Bolan considered what he had seen of Segawa and what he knew of Nenad. Surrendering to the Iranians just might be better than shooting each squad member to keep them all out of God's Army or the Serb's rape room.

It was a decision that he was going to have to make very soon.

Bolan rubbed his temples.

"I can do that for you," Von Kwakkenbos said.

It was indicative of how exhausted Bolan was that he hadn't heard the flight attendant's approach. She seemed to read Bolan's mind. "You're tired."

"I don't have time to be tired."

"You don't have time to run yourself ragged, either. We're all depending on you."

Von Kwakkenbos slid behind Bolan. Of its own will his body lay his head in her lap, and her fingers went to work on his temples. "How is Metard?"

"Sleeping. Like you should be."

Bolan changed the subject. "You did good today. You really helped Meat through the pain."

"I was very proud of Snake, she…" Von Kwakkenbos sighed.

"What?"

"The names, Meat, Snake, all that is happening. Being the loader on a machine-gun team. I am starting to feel much less a den mother and more like a little sister of a very dangerous fraternity."

"At least the food is good. Better than that airline stuff."

She made a noise. "Yes, Franco is a godsend. You are not so bad yourself."

Franco was a godsend. Captain Nenad was a thunderbolt straight out of Greek Tragedy, and Segawa had gone from a

Nemesis Bolan thought he just might elude to one arm of a trap that was about to snap shut.

“You need to sleep.”

“I rested on the boat.”

“You most certainly did not,” Von Kwakkenbos stated.

“I need to watch the river.”

“Franco is watching the river, and he is at least as good at it as you.”

Bolan could see some wisdom in that.

Von Kwakkenbos’s voice became serious. “I am not worried about you not being able to fight, Sergeant. I am worried about you becoming so tired that you make a mistake. We are all depending on you.”

That argument hit home. “I’m going to shut my eyes for a little while. Wake me up when the squad changes watch, if I’m not up already.”

“I promise, I will…” Von Kwakkenbos smiled in the night. The soldier was already asleep.

12

"Sarge?" Bolan was instantly awake. They had let him sleep until dawn. Sometime during the night, Bolan had gone from having his head pillowed to spooning. Rudipu looked more wistful than upset as he held out a cup of Franco's coffee. Pakzad stood beside him. "Franco says there are boats coming this way."

Bolan disentangled himself and rose to his feet. Von Kwakkenbos murmured in Afrikaans. *"Koffie..."* The brew of Congolese French roast was scalding hot and loaded with sugar. Bolan took several swallows and pressed the mug into the woman's hands. He took up his rifle. "Boats as in plural?"

"Franco thinks two, but he can't see them yet."

Bolan looked down at the camp. The problem with Franco's canoe was that it had been carved from a single tree trunk. It was far too heavy to drag out of the water and conceal. They had taken down the awning, then covered it with vines and branches, but the hide was going to fail even a cursory glance by anyone who had spent time on the river.

"Hammer!" Bolan shouted. "Form up! Rude, with me."

"Right, Sarge."

"Watch for crocs." Bolan moved down to the shoreline. He knelt in the reeds and broke open the grenade launcher he had taken from Pakzad. The bandolier of ammo was a standard combat load of mostly frags, two armor-piercing rounds, a flare round and a smoke.

"Here," Bolan handed Rudipu his binoculars. The Executioner front-loaded the weapon with the two armor-piercing rounds and backed it up with four frags.

"Here they come!" Rudipu whispered.

Bolan lowered his launcher and brought up his police rifle, frowning as the boats came into view in his scope. There were two of them. With their gaily painted, tropical theme awnings and white-painted rails, the two pontoon boats didn't look like they belonged in a small unit riverine action in the Congo. Bolan estimated they were twenty-four-footers.

Rudipu peered through Bolan's binoculars. "I think I rode on one of those at Disneyland last summer."

The men in the pontoon boats were long and far from Disney park cast members. They wore the universal Equatorial African uniform of shorts and donated T-shirts from the United States. Bolan noted that their assault rifles gleamed with that "out of the box" newness. It was very rare to see men with optics mounted on their rifles in this neck of Africa. Still rarer to see men actually deploy their weapons' folding stocks. The web gear they wore was still creased from storage. Handguns were a rare commodity in the Congo, yet each man wore a pistol on his web belt.

Rudipu picked up on the most disturbing anomaly. "Sarge, how come there are only three men in each boat? Each one could hold at least a squad."

"Why do you think, Rude?"

Rudipu saw it. "They're troop transports. Nenad sent them for Caesar."

"And?"

"And…" The cadet's brow bunched mightily. "Holy shit! He sent them ahead! If we let them get past, then we got Caesar on the water behind us. If we engage them, then Nenad knows exactly where we are!"

"So what do we do, Rude?"

"I don't like the idea of letting them get behind us and loading up with God's Army dipsticks, but engaging just six men in two boats is going to take up a lot of ammo, and I like

Nenad knowing where we are this morning even less. We let them pass if they discover us. Then we take them down."

"Your talents will be wasted in the Air Force, Rude." Bolan looked to Niner Squad. Johnson had them ready to deploy. Bolan called for a repeat of the glade massacre. "Cross fire, Hammer, and Huge on the pig down the middle. Get Meat out of sight and out of the line of fire."

Johnson looked out at the little hill beside the river and deployed his squad by fire teams. Pakzad replaced Metard on Jovich's fire team. Franco joined Johnson to reinforce the left flank. Hudjak and Pakzad carried the unconscious Metard in a blanket behind a deadfall on the extreme right and deposited him out of harm's way. Bolan and Rudipu waited in the reeds as the sound of diesels got louder.

The lead boat discovered the covered canoe almost instantly and turned toward the riverbank.

Bolan hadn't seen it going down any other way. "Here we go."

The men on board the boat scanned the shore intently. The other boat hung back in a fit of good sense. Its skipper was already on the horn to Nenad. Bolan aimed at the farther boat. Despite the awnings and fresh paint, the pontoon boats were old. The welded aluminum floatation cylinders were of single chamber construction rather than the more modern, safer, multichamber design.

Bolan fired.

The 40 mm high explosive round slammed into the starboard flotation chamber. The armor-piercing jet cut through the aluminum pontoon's skin like a hot knife through butter and filled it with superheated gas. The pontoon popped like a firecracker and the boat tipped. The two of the men screamed as they fell into the water. The man at the helm wheel shoved his throttle full forward to try to compensate. Rudipu's bullet put an end to his activities. The wheelman flopped from his chair and slid into the water.

The skipper of the lead boat hit his throttle and swerved away from the hillside. Niner Squad opened up. Bolan swung his launcher around and fired. The grenade hit the water and took a spectacular freak skip. The shaped-charge warhead detonated and sent a lance of white-hot fire through the air ten feet above the boat that hit nothing. Niner Squad hit the boat in a hail. One of the gunmen collapsed over the rail into the water. The other fell dead to the deck. Bolan fired again, and his grenade skimmed off the canopy and flew halfway across the river and plopped into the water. Bullets continued to riddle the boat, but the craft miraculously made it around the bend in the river and disappeared.

The first boat hung in the river by its surviving pontoon. Two men floated dead and bleeding in the water. Two other men screamed and clutched at the wreckage. It would have been a short swim to shore, but many people in the Congo didn't know how to swim and with good reason.

The crocodiles appeared out of nowhere.

The screaming ended abruptly as prehistoric reptiles spun and flailed their meals into crocodilian bite-size pieces. For a few brief seconds the brown water of the river ran red. The big crocs disappeared with their meals, while a few junior specimens cruised the blood slicks looking for leftovers. "I think I'm going to throw up," Rudipu said.

"Warned you about that, Rude."

To his credit Rudipu made a terrible swallowing noise and held his bile.

Johnson trotted up with a crestfallen look on his face. "Sorry, Sarge. He got away."

"No, Hammer. You got two, and he only got away because I missed. You have to Swiss cheese a pontoon boat to sink it with small arms. But he's leaking like a sieve with no way to patch up. He won't be transporting a squad of Caesar's men anywhere. Mission accomplished."

"Thanks, Sarge." Johnson grinned. "Your orders?"

"Take Huge, Ace and Donger. Get in the canoe with Franco. Catch up to that sinking boat. See if there's anything you can salvage. Make it quick." Bolan eyed several loglike objects with terrible, heavy-lidded eyes floating just beneath the surface of the river. "Watch out for crocs."

"Hey..." Everyone turned at the weak, plaintive little cry that came from behind the deadfall. Metard sat up blinking and looking around himself. "What'd I miss?"

"THEY'RE DEAD, Captain! Everyone is dead!" Nenad rolled his sunken eyes as his skipper, Sami, screamed across the phone. The Serbian gangster was far more interested in the GPS tracking device he held in his other hand. He had ten men in two speedboats, and they were proceeding east at a leisurely pace down the Nzoro. "Are you hurt?"

"What? I don't think so! I—"

"Was the other boat sunk?"

"Uhh..." Sami calmed a bit as his river pilot instincts took over. "No, Captain. The boat lost one pontoon and hung half-sunk by the other. It is most likely floating downriver."

Nenad watched the GPS screen. If the boat was moving, it was doing it so slowly that it didn't display. "Can you get to Caesar?"

"I can try, but the boat is badly out of trim. The starboard pontoon has been pierced repeatedly and is taking on water. I'll need a welder to repair it."

"Very well, Skipper. I do not believe you are being pursued. Stop at the first village you come to. Take the money I gave you and buy the two biggest canoes you can. Your outboards are clamp-ons. Attach them and vector Caesar and his men to your position, and bring them back west according to the original plan. Can you do that, Skipper?"

"Of course, Captain."

"Keep me updated."

Nenad punched another preset. "Captain Rhage?"

"Captain Nenad."

Nenad could hear an airplane taking off in the background. "May I inquire of your status?"

"My team is in the provincial capital. We are currently at Simi-Simi airport."

Nenad mulled over that bit of information. Nearly all commercial flights coming and going to Kisangani had been transferred to Bangoka International. Simi-Simi was almost exclusively a military airfield these days. The exceptions were expedited humanitarian flights and some rather hush-hush private operations. Operating out of Simi-Simi bespoke the amount of money the Iranians were pouring into this operation. "You have transportation?"

"I have arranged an Alouette III helicopter. I will be able to field a seven-man team. I have five more men with me. They will follow as a second team as soon as transportation can be arranged.

"How soon will your first team deploy?"

"Maintenance is often not what it could be in this part of the world, and the helicopter can be charitably described as well-used. We are fueling now, and my personal pilot is doing a preflight check. We should be airborne within the half hour. I predict a three-hour flight to your position, and we will be near the limit of our range. You have arranged for fuel?"

"I have a drum for you in each boat and a hand pump. You will be able to refuel. In case of an emergency there is more back at Nzoro."

"Excellent, we were able to smuggle in sidearms. You have weapons for us?"

Nenad glanced back at the crates in the back of his boat. "It's what I do."

"Very well, I will alert you when we are airborne, and you can vector us to your position."

"You should know that Caesar says one of your men is still alive, and is fighting alongside the American commando and the cadets."

Rhage paused. "I suspect this is simple survival on his part. I will need to speak to him. Remember, our aim is to take the cadets alive. I would like my man alive as well, at least long enough to explain himself."

"But of course."

"Speaking of taking them alive, you have what I requested of you?"

Nenad could not help but look back at his crates again. "Yes, and I cannot begin to tell you the expense it required." He did not bother to tell Rhage that he had a cache of the required items already in stock.

"You received monies wired to your offshore account in Mauritius?"

Nenad considered the ones and zeros that had appeared on his online account. "Indeed, more than ample."

"Until we meet."

Nenad clicked off. Once he stopped talking on the phone he could hear drums throbbing in the distance. The local Nzoro River grapevine was blowing up with calls. Nenad looked to his local expert. "Toko, I went to send a message upriver."

Toko flicked his cigarette into the river and took off his hat and shirt. The drummer cum gangster's frame was nothing but ebony muscle and bone. He clipped a microphone inside his talking drum and set his amplifier between the cockpit's two windscreens and turned the bass all the way up. "What shall I say, Captain?"

"Say anyone who helps the white devil heading west will feel my anger. Anyone caught with white children will suffer their fate. Anyone who comes to Nzoro with U.S. dollars will never trade there again."

Toko nodded. "You know if Franco is with them, he will translate for them."

"I am counting on it." Nenad's sunken eyes glittered. "Send a personal message to Franco. Tell him if he continues to help the white devil I will see to it that he dies in Caesar's fires. He can give them up at any time, and he will be rewarded." Nenad lit another cigarette. "Let us see if he translates that for them."

Toko put his drum between his knees and began pounding out a rapid rhythm of beats. The amplifier sent the message like thunder up the river. Nenad gazed steadily forward as if he could see the sound spreading his word. "Repeat the message on the hour for the next three hours."

Franco sobbed as his canoe was sent to the bottom of the river. Hudjak, Johnson, Jovich and King had jumped on it until the floor had cracked and broken. The rest of the squad piled rocks into the canoe and pushed it out into the stream. Bolan and Rudipu kept watch for crocodiles. Franco had understood, and agreed with the need to sink his vessel. They had to break contact with the enemy and find a new vector towards freedom. Another Islamic dinar helped assuage Franco's pain. Sentiment was still running high with the hunter, but the man's broken heart would mend. Bolan looked over at Metard—he was going to have to walk. Bolan strode over to him.

The young man was staring long and hard at the rounded, bandaged, tapered and missing-a-hand end of his left forearm. Field amputation was about as severe as surgery got. Bolan knew a vast number of vets, and he knew that amputees often went through severe depression. The soldier was pleased that the bandages at the amputation point were dry. Metard looked up and sighed in question. "Sarge?"

"So, you want to stick with Meat or go straight to Stumpy?"

Cadet Metard gave Bolan a very wan smile. "Given a choice, I'll stick with Meat, Sarge."

"Good man."

"Sarge?"

"Yeah?"

"Where's my hand?" Bolan held up a do-rag one of the squad had taken off the pontoon boat. The package was loosely tied, shapeless and about the size of a tennis ball. Metard blinked. He took the little bundle in his remaining hand. "You burned it?"

"Franco did it while you were sleeping. He even said some words over it while he did it," Bolan stated. "I thought you might like to scatter its ashes."

The cadet stared at the ashes of his hand. Metard was young. Bolan knew the healing of his arm and dexterity with a prosthesis would come with time, and most likely come quickly. Bolan needed Metard mentally over the loss effective immediately. The young man heaved a sigh. "Thank you, Sergeant."

Metard rose and walked toward the riverbank. Niner Squad ceased its activities and watched. The cadet stood staring out at the water. For a moment Bolan grimaced and thought he might have read the situation and the young man wrong. Metard squared his shoulders. He held the ashes in his remaining hand and pulled the loose knot of the kerchief open with his teeth. He spoke aloud as he slowly turned his hand over and ashes and small bones sifted into the river.

"Hand, we commend your ashes to the Democratic Republic of the Congo and the Nzoro. I thank you for your lifelong service, and we all thank you for your sacrifice to Niner Squad." Metard snapped the do-rag twice to get the last bits out of it and then on second thought chucked it into the river. He pulled his stump from his sling and gently waved it at the small, dispersing pattern of ash heading downriver. "I believe I speak for the rest of my constituent parts when I say we're all going to miss you, Lefty."

Johnson began clapping. "Fuckin' A, Meat!"

King joined in. "You're the man!"

The rest of Niner Squad began clapping, whistling and cheering. Metard walked back from the bank pale but grinning. Squad members gently pounded him on the back. Von Kwakkenbos and Shelby were both crying as they hugged him. Bolan spoke to Rudipu below the applause. "You might just have some competition on that presidential run of yours, Rude."

"That was incredible." Rudipu kept clapping. "You should change his name to Iron Balls, Sarge."

"Very brave," Pakzad said, as he clapped and leaned in. "You are a master of psychological warfare, Sergeant."

"More like master of inspired leadership," Rudipu said with a scowl. His eyes never left the Iranian operative for long. When they were encamped, Rudipu's rifle was always in a state of not quite pointed at the man. Bolan's sat phone vibrated in his pocket. "I'll be back in a minute."

He walked into the trees and answered. "What have you got for me, Bear?"

"The President and the senator are outraged you declined the Fulton STARS Extraction."

"I didn't decline it. Meat did."

"Meat?"

"And the entire squad, as well." Bolan left the amputation for discussion later. "What else you got?"

"Well, the interesting news is that Jack has gone AWOL."

"AWOL? Last I heard Jack was his own man."

Jack Grimaldi was Stony Man Farm's pilot. Long ago the crackerjack aviator had been operating on the wrong side of the law. Bolan had slapped him onto the right side of line, and the two men had been best friends ever since. He flew for Bolan. He flew for Able Team and Phoenix Force. He flew for the Farm, but like Bolan, Grimaldi was still an independent operator.

"Well, let's just say he's not around."

"He knows where I am and what the situation is?"

"I can't be sure," he said.

Bolan could imagine Kurtzman looking out at his cybernetic team. Carmen Delahunt, Huntington Wethers and Akira Tokaido would be paragons of virtue at their workstations, busily crunching data while they hung on Kurtzman's every word. Bolan heard someone shout. "But I think someone told him."

"Tell me Able and Phoenix aren't with him," Bolan said. His distant relationship with the United States government was well established. Able Team and Phoenix Force and the Farm worked far more specifically for it. Regardless, Bolan and the Farm operatives had crossed the line against official orders far more times than the soldier cared to think about. One of these days an angry chief executive just might flex his might against "loose cannons" and "rogue operators" and the crap was going to hit the fan. But a very real part of Bolan hoped Kurtzman would sigh and say yes, that they were on their way. Eight cadets, a flight attendant and Bolan himself were in desperate need of the cavalry.

"No," Kurtzman said. "Both teams are currently deployed on missions. They do not know your situation, and if they did we both know they would compromise the missions they are on for you. Jack knows that, too. Unless you were dead or captured, he wouldn't inform them just yet."

That was all too true. "How do you know he's missing?"

"Well, he's not answering his phone."

"And?"

"And Dragonslayer has gone missing."

A smile creased Bolan's face. Dragonslayer was one of the most interesting helicopters in existence and Grimaldi's pride and joy. "Isn't Africa just a little bit out of its range?"

"You know, you'd think that, but Jack has his ways."

Bolan felt a little glimmer of hope. "He's not answering your calls?"

"No."

The soldier thought Grimaldi might just answer his. "I'll get back to you, Bear." Bolan tapped off and punched in a number from memory. The line picked up in three rings. Bolan could hear the rumbling throb of turboprops in the background.

"Who is it?" Grimaldi asked sunnily.

"Jack..."

"Sarge?"

"Where are you?"

"On approach to the Azores," Grimaldi replied. "Where're you?"

"A northeastern corner of the DRC."

"I'd heard that."

"Didn't know Dragonslayer could reach the Azores without aerial refueling, buddy."

"It can't."

Bolan listened to the throbbing in the background. "Sounds like you're in a plane."

"You got good ears, Sarge."

"What are you flying?"

He paused for effect, as if he were a kid with his hand caught in the cookie jar. "Well, you know, a surplus C-130."

"Where's Dragonslayer?"

"In the back."

"Where'd you get a surplus C-130?"

"I know people in the surplus aircraft business, Sarge."

That was true and had come in handy in some remarkably unusual locations. "What'd you pay for it?"

"Well, you know."

"No, I don't."

"Ten mil. Well, ten and change," the pilot admitted.

"Where'd you get the money?"

"I borrowed it from a friend."

"You raided my war chests," Bolan stated.

"What?" Grimaldi's voice filled with mock indignation. "We're not friends? Besides, it was just one."

In Bolan's War Everlasting he had taken down some very big fish. Many of them kept very large amounts of money and liquid assets handy. Over the years he had stashed war chests in various places, including a large one in his quarters at Stony Man Farm.

"How's my plane?"

"It's a Hercules, baby!" Grimaldi enthused. "Until the day they invent antigravity engines, the design pretty much can't be improved upon."

"You alone?"

"Just me, myself and I!"

"What's your ETA?" Bolan asked.

Grimaldi became serious. "That's on you, Sarge. I am landing in Santa Maria, and when I take off I have genuine wonder as to where should I park this tub."

"The Iranians shot us down out of Sudan, and their HQ is Uganda. I'm assuming they have teams in the Orientale Province capital. Kisangani is out."

"Central African Republic?" Grimaldi surmised.

"That's how I figure it. How much money do you have left?"

He sounded more proud than contrite. "I got a lot!"

"I am going to forward you some names and numbers in the French Foreign Legion. The CAR is a hellhole, but the French have a real presence there. I have a few connections. You should be able to land and take off if you spread some money around."

"Way ahead of you." Grimaldi's voice dropped. "You got any more money?"

"How much do you need?"

"Well..." Grimaldi said, "how much instant-access assets do you have in Africa?"

"Why?"

"I'm on a solo mission, man! I didn't pack any weapons in case any politically motivated locals did a customs search. Right now Dragonslayer is listed in the manifest as a 'pleasure vehicle' destined for South Africa and it can pass that inspection. I'm going to have to buy a black-market weapons fit before I lift off."

"I'm sending you the name of a weapons dealer who will help you out. I'll send a password, so he'll know you're a friend. If you can't lift off out of the CAR fully armed with what he'll provide, you're on your own. He owes me his life, so money won't be a problem."

"'O ye of little faith...'"

"Jack, I gotta go."

"Copy that."

"Jack, get here as fast as you can."

Grimaldi's voice went serious again. "Copy that. Radio, phone or otherwise I will contact you with code name Freedom Train. If I use any other name, you will know we are compromised or at least being listened in on."

"Copy that, Freedom Train."

"I am landing and refueling. Will advise on extraction."

"Copy that." Bolan clicked off.

He called out to the squad. "We're marching!"

Johnson stood front and center. "Which way, Sarge?"

"North."

Eischen's camp comedian facade fell away. Everyone had seen Bolan talking on the phone. "Sarge?"

"Ace?"

"Do we have hope?"

"No." Bolan looked Cadet Eischen in the eye and told him the God's honest truth. "But as of now we have one desperate chance. March hard."

"Niner Squad!" Johnson shouted. "Get ready to move out!"

Niner Squad gathered up its gear. Von Kwakkenbos appeared at Metard's side to help him. He had stopped pushing her away, and she arranged his pack and his sling.

"Sarge?" Johnson appeared at Bolan's elbow.

"Yes, Hammer?"

"Well, I just, I mean…"

"You're doing fine, Squad Leader."

Johnson grinned sheepishly. "That's not what I meant. I just wanted to say thank you."

"For?"

"For dropping in. For everything. I mean, none of us want to be here. We all want to go home."

Bolan saw where this was going. "But…?"

"Sarge, I know we're just kids, but we signed up to be soldiers. This is the shit. This is the classroom of all classrooms." Johnson struggled to put his thoughts into words. "I mean, except for letting Ace fire the flare—"

"It's okay, Hammer…"

"Yeah, well..." Hammer suddenly stood tall. "I mean. Whenever you and Rude go off on sniper team, and I'm really leading the squad, every decision I make, before I make it, I ask myself, what would the sarge do? I think I'm getting better at it." There was no defense against Cadet Johnson's absolute earnestness. "I think I'm going to be asking myself that question for rest of my military career, and I wanted to say thanks."

"Sucking up, Hammer?"

Johnson shook his head. "Sorry, Sergeant. That's my story, and I'm sticking to it."

"Hammer, get the Squad moving."

14

Bolan watched the village from behind the tall grass.

Johnson, Rudipu and Pakzad lay with him. Niner Squad had spent the past forty-eight hours marching hard for the CAR. They were far from the savannah, much less the desert, but as they moved northward the rain forest sometimes opened into grassy, rolling hills, and at the top of them you could occasionally feel the hot, sand-smelling wind driven by the convection caldron of the Sahara. They forded two rivers in four days and had come upon the village midmorning. It was another break in the rain forest. The break had been expanded and cleared for the villagers' fields. Many of the traditional thatched huts had given way to corrugated iron shanty sheds. Many more were hybrids of the two. Women were spreading cassava chips to dry on reed mats. Men fished in the river with nets.

Franco smacked his lips.

The late-afternoon breeze carried the scent of something bubbling in the cook pots, and whatever was for dinner smelled good. The squad's dwindling diet of cold *fufu* dough and dried meat from Franco's stash was getting awfully thin, and while it lasted Bolan had put the emphasis on marching rather than hunting. Of far more interest to him was the dirt road that led from the village into a break in the forest, and the old French Simca Cargo flatbed truck parked in the village square.

One of the larger, low rambling constructions had a satellite dish.

"Something isn't quite right," Johnson opined.

"And what might that be, Squad Leader?"

"They're in the middle of nowhere, but they have a truck, a satellite dish and a lot of other stuff subsistence fishermen and farmers in this part of the DRC shouldn't have the wherewithal to own."

"So?" Bolan prompted.

Johnson scanned the rain forest just beyond the burn line of the village fields. "They're growing themselves something besides plantains up in those hills, Sarge."

"So tell me why they need a truck."

"Well...rivers are the highways around here." Johnson considered the dirt track leading into the trees, then nodded as he saw it. "That's a logging road."

"Bring it home, Hammer."

"They're running poached logs downstream. No army, police or gangster wants to hijack a load of logs going down-river and ride herd on it for two weeks. They let the villagers do that and charge them for the privilege along the way. But a boat load of pot? That they would flat out steal. The village runs poached logs down the river and uses the logging roads like moonshiners use back roads to bring the supply directly to their distributor and cut out a lot of the middlemen on the river."

Rudipu grinned. "No wonder he made you squad leader."

"And what do we take from all this, General?"

Johnson's brow furrowed. "Captain Nenad knows about this village. He probably does business with it, at least through middlemen."

"So ends the lesson."

"So what do we do, Sarge?" Rudipu asked.

Pakzad smiled. "Yes, Sergeant. What is our plan?"

"I don't want to try to sneak around the village by day—too much exposure, and I don't want to waste energy trying to go around this line of hills. We wait until dusk. No one goes out at night in this part of the Congo. We'll rest now, and then use the night-vision goggles to sneak past and do some night walking."

Pakzad sighed. “Why don’t we just take the truck?”

“Because if they’re running cannabis and illegal logging, they’re most likely armed. We can’t afford a firefight, and I don’t want one. We got lucky with Meat losing a hand. One leg or torso wound, and we’re carrying a litter and our marching days are over. Plus if we take the truck and get away? Between Nenad and Caesar, that village is going to get crushed. We wait and—” Bolan’s head snapped and he looked towards the southwest sky.

Rudipu cocked his head. “Rotors, Sarge?”

“Back to the trees.” They loped down the low hill and ran for the cover of the green wall a hundred yards ahead. They crashed through the underbrush as a chopper flashed overhead. Bolan turned and watched the bottle green helicopter orbit the village. Women rolled up their sorting mats and men ran from the river. Other men came out of the habitations with guns. The chopper came to a landing beside the logging road about fifty yards from the village. Men hopped out of the helicopter as it powered down. Bolan scanned through his optics. Two of the men were Caucasian, one was black, and the other four looked Middle Eastern. The white and the black men waved to the villagers and they waved back. The pilot and one gunman stayed with the chopper but stretched their legs outside and began smoking.

“Do you recognize them?” Pakzad asked. At this distance without optics, the Iranian operative wasn’t able to make out much other than the shapes of men deploying. Bolan decided not to let the sergeant major know that some of his friends had arrived.

“Bad guys.”

“Ah.”

Johnson lowered his binoculars. “Does this alter the plan, Sarge?”

“Oh, yeah.”

“What do we do?”

“I want you to get me Huge’s cleanest T-shirt and that fatigue cap Ace is wearing, and bring whatever's left of the toiletries. Oh, and bring me a pack of Franco's cigarettes."

"Okay."

"Switch guns with me."

Johnson took Bolan's rifle and submachine gun and handed over his Kalashnikov. "Sarge, what's going on?"

Bolan pointed to some bare hilltops a few miles northwest of the village. "If you push hard, you can get there in an hour, hour and a half."

"What are you going to do?" Johnson asked.

"Hope our friends have been flying all morning and are going to take a meeting with the village elders, stretch their legs and have a late lunch."

The sly grin on Johnson's face said he already knew the answer to his next question. "And then?"

"And then I'm going to try something really stupid."

BOLAN FINISHED SHAVING. He'd done it with his combat knife and a travel-size packet of Von Kwakkenbos's facial moisturizer, but he had managed not to cut himself. He used some moist towelettes to clean up his cargo pants as best he could. The last of the soap got most of the blood and grime off his hands and arms. Hudjak's T-shirt was white and clean. Bolan pulled it on and set Eischen's fatigue cap on his head at a jaunty angle. He put one of Franco's cigarettes between his lips and rolled the pack in the left sleeve of his shirt.

Bolan dropped a dime on Johnson and peered through the trees. It had been an hour and fifteen minutes. The men from the chopper had gone into the biggest house. A village woman had just come out and brought the chopper pilot and his guard some food. It was time.

"Hammer, where are you?"

Johnson was breathing hard. "Be there in ten..."

"Copy that." Bolan lit his smoke and walked out onto the logging road. He carried his AK over his shoulder by the barrel like he didn't have a care in the world. The soldier blew smoke and pretended to be talking into his cell phone as he walked toward the chopper. The pilot and the guard sat on the edge of the open cabin and spoke to each other in Farsi around mouthfuls of chicken and rice. A French AAT machine gun hung by chicken straps between them. They took far too long to notice Bolan. When they did, they nearly strangled on their food and hopped up. The Executioner kept walking forward and waved his phone at them. Bolan faked a very thick and indeterminate accent around his smoke. "Hey! Boss! You speak English?"

The pilot's hand went to his holster. The guard seemed to be considering whether to unsling his rifle. "Who are you?"

"Bruno. Hey, listen, Captain Nenad's truck. It's kaput, about ten klicks back up the road."

"What truck?"

"Listen! Radio Nenad!" Bolan waggled his phone again. "No fucking reception." Bolan stepped within range.

The guard shook his head. "We need to—"

Bolan swung the Kalashnikov off his shoulder and whipped it up like a polo mallet. The guard's teeth flew. The pilot gaped for one second. It was plenty of time for Bolan to kick a field goal right between the uprights, and the pilot collapsed vomiting and clutching himself. The village seemed not to have noticed the mostly silent violence fifty yards away. That was except for a couple of kids who came running out from between two structures chasing a soccer ball. They were facing the chopper and stopped and stared at the man with the rifle in his hands and the two men lying on the ground.

Bolan waved.

One of the kids waved back.

The other ran back the way he had come.

The soldier clambered into the cockpit and slid into the pilot's seat. The chopper was an Alouette III and looked like it had seen a lot of hard use. The fuel gauge showed a quarter tank. That told Bolan that Nenad was most likely fairly close by, probably on the river and carrying fuel in his boats. He hit the starter button. The turbine shaft above groaned and began to turn. Bolan slowly shoved his throttle forward as the rotors began to beat against the air.

Men began running out of the big house and adjoining huts to see what was going on. Bolan decided not to wait for the rotors to come up to speed. He jumped out of the cockpit and into the backseat. Men began pointing, while some jumped up and down. The helicopter's crew began running forward with pistols drawn. Bolan jumped into the back and got his hand around the grip of the door gun. Villagers, Serbian gangsters and Iranian gunmen threw themselves down as Bolan cut loose. He stitched lines across the rooftops, shaving close to the men on the ground, and put a nice long burst into the grille of the truck. The belt spit out its last cartridge case, and Bolan dropped the smoking machine gun on its strap. He jumped out of the cabin and back into the cockpit. Men began to stand as Bolan rammed the throttle forward. The helicopter rose and Bolan kicked the collective. The chopper spun and skimmed bare yards above the earth to put the hill he had observed from the village between him and the gunmen. The Alouette III was not a gunship. It was a lovely thing, but a lovely machine made of aquarium-worthy expanses of glass, and it had a thin metal frame.

Bolan heard a few bullets hit the fuselage, but no alarms went off and no power or control was lost. He got the hill between him and the pursuing small-arms fire. He banked hard dangerously close to the wall of the rain forest and spent anxious seconds in the open as he made for the river. The range was close to a thousand yards, and no more bullets rattled against the chopper's thin hide.

The soldier reached the river and used the corridor of trees on either side to obscure his escape. The Alouette threw up a rooster tail of brown water as Bolan flew nap of the river. He traveled about a klick, rose into the air and took the chopper a few yards above the jungle canopy. He began his wide circle around the village to get to the hilltop where Niner Squad was supposed to be waiting.

"ARRIAN HAS A BROKEN jaw." Medhi was the light support weapon man on Rhage's team and also the medic. Captain Rhage thought the state of Arrian's dental health was pretty damn obvious but he held his tongue. Haghigi howled as Arrian pressed a couple of fingers low beneath the man's belt line. Medhi sighed. "I am a medic as opposed to a medical doctor, but I believe Haghigi had a herniated testicle."

Sami didn't understand Farsi but had seen Medhi's prodding and looked away diplomatically.

Rhage was just about ready to live up to his name's English homonym. He felt like shooting his team and burning the village. Rhage could accept defeat. He could accept living to fight another day. Indeed compared to many Iranian special forces soldiers he was absolutely willing to lose a thousand battles if in the end it won the war. He was Quds Force. That was the nature of his business. But this was outright humiliation. The American had walked out of the jungle, beaten two of his men useless and stolen his helicopter.

Rhage would have kicked Haghigi's other testicle up into his tonsils but even he had to admit that Haghigi was currently paying a steep price for his failure. "Can you reduce it?"

The captain spent most of his time being dangerously reasonable. However, his men knew from long experience exactly when they were in danger. Unfortunately, Medhi had gone the way of a medic with a patient, and he was currently invulnerable to intimidation. "Captain, your men need immediate medical attention."

Rhage shoved his fury aside and spoke in French. "Sami, please call Captain Nenad."

Sami punched a few buttons. He gave Rhage an inscrutable look and spoke in Isoro. Rhage nearly shot him. After Sami briefed Nenad, he smiled at Rhage, nodded and spoke French as he handed him the phone. "The captain, Captain."

"Captain," Rhage said.

"I understand you have run into some trouble," Nenad replied.

Rhage's knuckles went white, but his tone remained neutral. "The American has stolen our helicopter."

"Of what matter is that?"

That took Rhage off guard. "What do you mean?"

"How many men does an Alouette III hold?"

Rhage suddenly felt a great weight off his chest. "Seven."

"And how many must the American carry?"

Something else filled Rhage's chest. "Currently twelve."

"And how do Americans feel about leaving anyone behind?"

"In my experience it is nearly mythological as to the Herculean efforts and resources the Americans will expend to bring back all their men, living, wounded or dead."

"He has denied us the use of one helicopter. Good for him. Emotionally flawed as Americans are, they are still amazing soldiers. But their code is a two-edged sword. He is alone, and the back edge cuts him with every decision he makes. I am tempted to say his acts are becoming increasingly desperate. And your second team is on the way in the second helicopter. Their ETA to my position is forty-five minutes, but they will require refueling. I am currently about an hour away from your position downriver. Caesar is not on the same river as us but it is parallel, and, if nothing else, Caesar and his people can scamper through the jungle for days at a time. Dusk is coming. I believe everything will converge quite nicely." Nenad laughed. "Do not worry, Captain. It is my belief that tomorrow the Americans will be ours."

15

Niner Squad jumped up and down and waved as Bolan brought the chopper in to land. The squad was camped on an open spot on the hillside. A spring filled a hot-tub-size pool and then overflowed to keep cascading down the hill. Bolan landed. The whooping and cheering became audible as he throttled down and cut power to the turbine. He grabbed the tool kit and hopped out, crouching as he moved out from under the rotors. Von Kwakkenbos planted a wet kiss on his cheek. Bolan excused the lapse in discipline. Johnson cocked his head at the bird and immediately saw the problem. "Sarge, there're only seven seats."

"Yeah." Bolan nodded. He gazed long and hard at the French helicopter as the rotors slowed and stopped. Math was a harsh mistress. The Alouette III carried three up front in the cockpit and four passengers in the cabin. Bolan needed to get a twelve-man squad airborne. He could currently account for seven. He handed Johnson the tool kit. "Lose the seats. Huge, help him."

Johnson and Hudjak took the wrenches and began busting knuckles on the bolts.

"All except the pilot's. I'm gonna need that," Bolan advised. "Then lose the doors." Bolan knew it was far from enough. "Snake, Ace, anything inside and out that isn't nailed down."

Eischen combed the inside and began hurling out detritus. It wasn't much and got increasingly pathetic. Bolan winced as he lost the French AAT. He would have loved to hold on to the door gun, but he needed to lose every ounce of its twenty-two pounds. Eischen tossed the fire extinguisher and all the headsets except the pilot's. He was quickly reduced to maps, pens and wires that seemed nonessential. Shelby snapped off the windshield wipers, two external antennas and the chin-mounted air probe. Bolan pulled a wrench out of the tool kit and tossed it to Rudipu. "Climb on top. Take off the engine housing. Unbolt everything that doesn't seem to be a moving part. While you're at it lose every body panel that bolts on. Jock-itch, help him."

"Right!"

Bolan watched the turbine cowling and the upper fuselage panels strip away. Niner Squad crawled across the chopper inside and out like army ants chewing their way across a carcass.

Von Kwakkenbos stepped beside Bolan. "Will it fly?"

"No, not yet."

"Then we must choose—"

"We leave no one behind." Bolan watched Hudjak toss aside the small pilot's side door and wipe his brow. "You're losing the pig, Huge. You're a maggot now."

"Sarge?"

"In the United States Army Rangers, which you have claimed to aspire to, pigs carry machine guns and support weapons. Maggots are riflemen. You're a maggot like the rest of us now, Huge."

Hudjak cocked his leonine head. "Is this a demotion, Sarge?"

"No, Huge. We're just trying to lighten your overgrown ass. Hand over your weapon."

"Right, Sarge." Hudjak handed over his Russian machine gun.

Bolan examined the naked and gutted helicopter. Short of dumping fuel, there was only one place left to lose any real weight. "Everyone go stand behind the chopper." Niner Squad obeyed while Bolan fished one of the gas masks out of a pack. He strapped it on to protect his eyes and face and stepped into the cabin. He crouched and held the weapon in the hip assault position. The Alouette's cockpit was a greenhouselike bubble of six sweepingly curved windscreens with thin metal frame in between. Bolan began giving each pane a long burst. Bits of flying glass pricked Bolan's forearms and smacked against the mask he wore as he fired. He kept firing until the machine gun spit out the last spent shell casing and oozed smoke on empty. The front of the chopper was a Swiss-cheesed mess of bullet holes and an opaque spiderweb of cracks. Bolan clambered out and stripped off his mask "Huge, Jock-itch. Kick out the panels. Ace, Snake, clean the frames with a hammer or a wrench. Then sweep the broken glass off the cabin and cockpit floors."

The cadets began kicking out sagging windscreen panels and running tools along the frames to take out the toothlike remnants. Bolan took a lap around the bird. Every removable body panel was gone, exposing the birds guts. Nothing remained inside other than the pilot's seat and the controls. With the doors and windows gone, the cockpit and cabin were empty, skeletal frames. The chopper seemed to look at Bolan accusingly.

"Will it fly?" Von Kwakkenbos asked.

"It might just," Bolan replied. "Donger, word is you're an Eagle Scout. It's going to be a bumpy ride. I want you to string a rope on both sides of the fuselage as a safety rail. Then string two on the inside. One stem to stern and one port to starboard across the middle. I want people to have something to hold on to, and I want it secure."

"On it, Sarge!" King took his *panga* and the coil of rope and went Eagle Scout on the gutted bird. Bolan took out his knife and began cutting away the filters and the bottom part of his gas mask, leaving just the goggles. "Everyone, one weapon. Six mags. Keep the grenades. Ditch the rest." Bolan tossed the spent machine gun into the pool, followed by his South African police pistol. The squad tossed the submachine guns and pistols and kept their rifles.

King leaned out of the chopper. He plucked his ropes and they thrummed taut. "Ready, Sarge!"

Bolan checked his watch. He didn't think the Iranians would march on him this late in the day, but Julius Caesar Segawa and his men were another story. "Everyone eat as much of the food as you can now. We're losing the rest. Then take a dump and take a leak. We are blowing ballast."

Niner Squad tore open the last of the packaged French rations. Bolan figured if they didn't make it across an international border, he and Franco could hunt down something. "Sarge!" King tossed Bolan a tiny tin of pâté. "You gotta eat!"

Bolan caught it and pulled back the tab. It was barely three mouthfuls, but it was pure protein and fat. Marching food. Bolan took the entire tin with two fingers. He savored it for a moment and swallowed. "Thank you, Donger."

"You're welcome, Sarge!"

"Niner Squad, mount up! Rude, you are going to be the chopper's shooter! Donger! Put a rope around his waist but give him enough slack to move to both sides of the cabin. Then put the same on Huge. Huge! You are Rude's real safety strap. God help you if I see Rude dangling beneath the chopper. You are going to take hold of the back of his belt and never let go. You read me?"

Rudipu, Hudjak and King sounded off. "Copy that, Sarge!"

"Meat only has one hand! Whoever is next to him, on both sides, wrap yourself around one of the security ropes and wear him like underwear. This ride is going to get rough."

Von Kwakkenbos moved to Metard's side. Eischen sidled up to the other. "Gonna wear you like underwear, bitch."

Metard lifted his stump out of his sling. "I will shove this up your ass, Ace."

Eischen grinned at Bolan. "We're all good here, Sarge!"

Bolan hit the button.

King deployed rope. Niner Squad huddled onto the steel pallet that had once been a helicopter. Metard sat in the middle of the back. Von Kwakkenbos and Eischen wound their arms into ropes and took firm hold of their charge. Everyone else piled in. Safety ropes were tied to Rudipu and Hudjak. Rudipu crouched midcabin with his Dragunov. Hudjak took a fistful of Rudipu's belt at the small of his back and another handful of rope.

Bolan reached up and shoved the throttle forward.

Shelby had tied some rope to the pilot's position and sat at Bolan's elbow. Pakzad sat next to her and held on to the rail rope King had slung along the side. Bolan pulled his makeshift goggles down over his eyes and pushed the throttle all the way forward. He muttered under his breath.

The helicopter skeleton rose about a foot. It bumped its wheels against rocks and slid sickeningly across the tiny plateau like a week-old birthday balloon that was a whisper away from negative buoyancy. The throttle handle stopped against the top of the slots. The turbine howled and hurricanes whipped through the empty cockpit, door and window frames.

The chopper wasn't going anywhere.

Franco began shouting from the back. Bolan looked over his shoulder. "What's he saying?"

Pakzad shouted over the rotor noise. "Franco says you can leave him! Alone he thinks he has a decent chance of eluding Caesar!"

Bolan looked at Franco. The old hunter gave him a very sad smile in return. Franco would be a hunter in the Congo without a boat, and with Segawa and Nenad as enemies. He would be a hunter who was the hunted. Even with the money Bolan had given him, he would not be able to counter the price on his head. With his skills he might well be able to live a few more years in the wilderness, but it would be a lonely life, and short. Never again would Franco tie up his boat at a village or town and haggle over his wares. He would never again go to a *nganda* bar, drink a beer and shoot the bull with the other hunters and watch the girls go by. He would never go to church again or have a roof over his head. He would die alone, or more likely in the end die caught.

"Tell Franco he's Niner Squad! We don't leave anyone behind!"

Pakzad translated. Franco started crying again. Bolan returned his attention to his controls and tried to figure out how to lose more weight. Maybe if they all stripped naked. Maybe if they all induced vomiting, maybe if pigs could fly…

"Sergeant!" Pakzad said.

"Yeah!"

"On a personal note, I weigh fifty-four point five kilograms! I do not consider myself a member of your squad, and I am perfectly willing to jump out of this aircraft!"

Bolan considered the Quds operative's offer. Pakzad knew every aspect of the squad, their weapons, their health, their food supply, the state of the helicopter, and there was no promise Bolan could force out of the operative that he would keep once he linked up with his people. The obvious answer was to blow his brains out and shove him over the side. He glanced back. "Hammer?"

"He kept his word, Sarge. I say so do we. Cut him loose."

Bolan nodded. The die was cast. Niner Squad was going to live or die with honor. "Give up your gear."

"You would leave me alone with nothing in the jungle?"

"You can keep your canteen and your pistol. You'll meet up with your own soon enough."

"Fair enough."

"Pakzad?"

"Yes?"

Bolan leaned over. Only he, Pakzad and Shelby could hear him. "You unload that pistol into this helicopter on your way out, and you know what I'll do to you."

Pakzad looked back steadily into Bolan's eyes. "You and I shall part as friends. When next we meet, we are enemies."

The Executioner nodded. Pakzad lost his pack and his silenced submachine gun. He took a long last look around the squad and smiled.

"Until we meet again," Pakzad said, and then he stepped out of the chopper. Rudipu kept his weapon aimed at him.

The chopper began to rise.

The Alouette III fought for every foot of altitude. Pakzad

waved. Bolan turned the helicopter and took it off the hill and over the trees. Going downhill gave him a little momentum to work with, but the chopper was so heavily overloaded that the momentum itself was a danger. Von Kwakkenbos screamed as one of the nonretractable wheels hit something green and the Alouette lurched. Shelby tossed Pakzad's submachine gun and magazines out into the greenery. His pack followed it. The chopper gained a few almost imperceptible increments of lift. Flying the grossly overloaded and out-of-trim chopper was like trying to ride a pig across a river and about as easy to steer.

Bolan's flying pig was squealing over every foot and fought him all the way.

CAPTAIN RHAGE CURSED God. He watched through his binoculars as his stripped chopper wobbled into the sky. "Sami, get Nenad on the phone."

Sami pointed to the river. "The captain is here."

Two speedboats appeared at the bend in the river and sliced up to the village piers. Rhage bellowed and pointed to the sky. "Captain!"

Nenad squinted from the cockpit of his boat and raised his binoculars just in time to see the Alouette III slide out of sight over the rain forest canopy. Rhage and Sami ran to the pier. Nenad lowered his binoculars and nodded. "Yankee ingenuity. I would have simply shot your man and Franco and pushed them out."

Rhage narrowed his eyes at the Serbian gangster.

Sami's eyes widened, and he pointed south towards the green wall of rain forest. Armed men streamed out of the jungle in platoon strength. Rhage clenched his fists. Nenad's "nice convergence" had come just a little too late. He watched Segawa and his men jog up with a mixture of awe and repugnance. He had worked in Africa for a number of years and he knew from experience how out of hand things could get. But Caesar Segawa and his men took the horror show to a new level. Rhage was appalled when he saw the woman running with them, and he was horrified when she smiled at him to reveal her mouth of filed teeth.

It reinforced Rhage's belief in the Islamic Revolution. Only Sharia law could stamp out such animals.

Segawa seemed to read the Quds Force officer's mind. "Heard you lost your helicopter."

Nenad broke in as Rhage bristled. "Caesar, where is my skipper?"

Segawa turned his pinhole pupiled eyes on Nenad. "Your man couldn't keep up."

Nenad did not seem particularly concerned.

Rhage was deeply concerned. "Our quarry flies away as we speak."

"The American flaps like an injured bird. He goes neither far nor fast."

Everyone looked up at the sound of rotor noise in the south. Another helicopter approached over the hills. The dark blue chopper was big, with two engines and a large, cargo and troop-carrying cabin. The Aérospatiale Puma came in for a landing. The cabin doors were locked open. The sight of the side-firing 20 mm cannon pleased all assembled. Rhage's pilot Farshid had outdone himself. It was amazing what the right amount of jingling piles of Islamic dinars could do. Rhage was forced to admit that he was more of a strategist than a tactician. "Captain, what is your proposed plan?"

"Simple. We can catch them easily before sundown. We put a squad of Caesar's men into the cabin. You and I and some picked men will ride up front. Obua will lead the rest of Caesar's legion on foot behind us," Nenad said. "They will catch up with us after we force the Americans down."

"There is a chance many of them would die."

Nenad gave a fatalistic shrug. "The cadets have already survived one crash. There is every reason to believe many of them would survive another. Besides, I did not say shoot them down, I said force them down. Their helicopter can barely fly. It should be quite easy to maneuver them into a position they know is helpless, particularly with the cannon."

"And if they refuse?"

"Then shoot them down and let the cards fall where they may. It is my opinion that none of them should be allowed to leave the DRC alive or dead."

Mama Waldi exposed her teeth. "Should they all die in a crash, there shall be a feast unknown for decades."

Segawa dipped the tip of his knife into the little bag of mystery leather around his neck. He took a snort and nodded at Mama Waldi's wisdom. "Truth."

Rhage would have drawn his pistol and shot them both, but he was badly outnumbered at the moment. He looked to Nenad. The Serb seemed excited about Mama Waldi's proposition.

"And should they survive?"

Segawa shoved forth his hand like an emperor making a decree. "The spoils have been divided. The money and the dark children go to Nenad. The white children shall cleave unto me. Obua shall be rewarded with the whore of apartheid."

Rhage eyed the drug-addled fanatic before him. "Forgive me, Caesar, but why are I and my men here then?"

"You shall have the White Leopard. Nenad and I have discussed this. We think he may know many things your supreme leader would be interested in."

"This is true, but I believe he is willing to die to protect his charges."

"And by the same token, when forced down, he will surrender himself in hopes of saving them."

"How?"

Nenad answered. "You will tell him that you have offered me vast amounts of money, and Caesar great caches of guns for the right to take the cadets to Iran and the supreme leader. By the way, this will be true, in recompense for our cooperation."

"I see your logic, but why would he believe this?"

Mama Waldi showed Rhage the gleaming, filed points of her dentition. "Because he will have no choice. While there is life there is hope. You will make it clear to him that if he refuses his children fall to us. With you there will be hope of ransom or prisoner exchange. It is a deal he will have to take, and pray that it is true."

"Meanwhile," Nenad concluded, "in my boat I have that which we discussed. There is every chance should they survive being forced down we can take them with or without the American's agreement."

"Then we are all in agreement," Rhage said.

"Good. Sami, unload two barrels of fuel and the pump."

The fuel drums were manhandled off the pier and rolled onto the landing green. Rhage watched the sun slowly begin to fall from the sky with increasing trepidation. Refueling a helicopter with a hand pump was a maddeningly slow process. Sami pointed north. Rhage's eyebrows rose as Sergeant Major Pakzad came running out of the trees. He beelined toward his commanding officer. Rhage waved a hand at the gasping sergeant major as he saluted. "Catch your breath, Pakzad. Take a little water."

Water spilled down Pakzad's chin as he gulped from a canteen. He put his hands on his knees and gasped for a few moments and stood. Rhage nodded. "Report."

"You saw the Americans take off?"

"Indeed we did, Sergeant Major."

"It is the commando, the flight attendant, the hunter Franco and the eight cadets. The helicopter has been stripped down to its bones. It can fly but only just. They are down to less than a quarter tank of fuel."

"Anything else pertinent?"

"They have abandoned nearly all of their equipment to save weight, and all except the commando are down to one weapon and six magazines. The senator's son, Metard, was injured and had to have his hand amputated. I cannot confirm it, but I believe they are heading for the Central African Republic."

Rhage, Nenad and Segawa all looked at one another. The operative, the gangster and the revolutionary were all in agreement. Rhage nodded at Pakzad. "Take a little food. We take off as soon as the chopper is fueled."

16

The sun was sinking fast. The Alouette's fuel gauge was dropping into the red at nearly the same pace. The helicopter was barely doing sixty miles per hour. The constant buffeting inside the chopper and the uninsulated roar of the engine had beaten most of the squad into a nonrestful doze with their hands still white-knuckled in sleep around the safety ropes. Shelby clutched Bolan's pilot's seat and slept with her head against his leg. She looked up yawning and blinking as the helicopter lurched. She squinted into the wind and suddenly sat up in alarm. "Sarge!"

"I see it!"

Bruised clouds swept toward them out of the north. The daily downpour was running late this day. Shelby's head whipped around what was left of the chopper. "I don't suppose we can climb above it?"

"You maintain that sense of humor, Snake!" Bolan shouted. "You're going to need it! Wake everyone up! Tell them to hold on!"

The skies opened, and the rain and the straining helicopter closed with each other. Niner Squad blinked awake and clutched the ropes for their lives. Bolan flew Niner Squad into a car wash in a convertible at sixty miles an hour. The inside of the chopper instantly became a washing machine on spin cycle. The engine howled as Bolan kept it at full throttle. Rain hissed off the overheating metal, and water rushed into parts of the helicopter that were never intended to get wet. The helicopter slowly and perceptibly began to lose altitude.

Rudipu howled in the maelstrom. “Sarge!”

Bolan turned to look.

A dark blue Aérospatiale Puma helicopter pulled up next to the Alouette III like a police car pulling them over. The 20 mm Giat cannon pointed at them was telling them to set down. The cabin of the Puma was full of armed men. A hulking, skull-faced individual who could only be Captain Nenad pointed his finger downward for emphasis.

Rudipu’s voice rose in panic as he aimed his rifle back. The young man was feeling a little outgunned. “Sarge?”

Bolan saw Pakzad wave at him, and he also got his first real good look at Julius Caesar Segawa and his lady friend, and he didn’t like what he saw. The Puma was equipped with a public-address system, and it blared over the rotors and rain. “Throw your weapons out of the aircraft! Slow to fifty kilometers per hour and follow us to the next clearing!”

Bolan glanced at his fuel gauge and back at the 20 mm automatic cannon. There was a slash of river ahead cutting the canopy, but it was too narrow to make a landing. Bolan was glad his goggles masked his facial expression. Shelby looked up at him. Rain ran down her face in wind-whipped rivulets, but Bolan could tell by her expression that none of them were tears. “Sarge?”

“Yeah!”

“I think I speak for the squad when I say I would rather be a smoking hole in the canopy than fall into those people’s hands.”

“Yeah, me, too!” Bolan yanked his stick hard over and forward. “Hold on!”

The chopper tipped precipitously and slid right beneath the Puma. Overloaded as she was there was only one thing she could do well and that was fall from the sky like stone. Bolan shoved his stick all the way forward and dived for the river. “Niner Squad! Open fire! Full-auto!”

The interior of the Alouette was cramped with bodies but without windows or doors there were plenty of firing ports. Muzzles thrust awkwardly out of the empty frames and Kalashnikovs ripped into life as the Puma banked after them. Bolan brought the Alouette screaming down for the deck. He took a page out of Flight Officer Pieter Llewellyn's playbook and decided to use the river as his runway. "Brace for impact!"

The Alouette swept down a far too short, straight stretch of river and promptly snapped off her main rotors. The chopper hit the water and skipped like a stone borne upon the wings of momentum. God could not have given them a better second hit. The tail rotors dipped into the water and acted like a drag chute. Only the safety ropes kept Niner Squad from flying through the empty cockpit window frames. The main fuselage hit the water and fountained up through the empty chin windows. Screams filled the chopper as the Alouette stood on its empty nose and promptly began sinking.

"Rifles, gear and get out!" Bolan shouted.

The tail fell back into the water, and the river was instantly up to Bolan's knees. King had his *panga* out already. He cut Rudipu and Hudjak free of their safety ropes and slashed the starboard rope rail. Niner Squad piled out and began swimming for shore. Metard nearly went under as he tried to keep his stump and his rifle above the muddy water. Von Kwakkenbos hooked him in an efficient lifeguard rescue tow and kicked shoreward. Bolan clicked out of his straps, and Johnson handed him his weapons and web gear. The cadet then dived into the river and swam to assist Von Kwakkenbos. Bolan turned at the sound of the Lord's Prayer in French. Franco was clutching the fuselage frame, babbling in mindless terror and seemed ready to go down with the ship. He had spent his entire life on the rivers of the Congo and like any Congolese native with an ounce of sense he had avoided ever going into it deeper than two feet and only then under duress. Bolan shoved his rifle and submachine gun into Franco's hands. The man stared at the weapons uncomprehendingly as the water went up to their chests.

Franco shrieked as Bolan hooked him beneath the armpits and did a drowning man rescue tow. To Bolan's infinite relief Franco mindlessly clutched the weapons in his hands rather than him. The soldier managed to keep both their heads above water. He felt hands grabbing his shoulders and his boots hit mud as Hudjak and Eischen helped pull him and his suddenly limp burden ashore. A hurricane blasted the river into a white squall as the Puma circled low. The little river was far too narrow for the Puma to make any kind of landing. It seemed they had not brought fast ropes with them nor did anyone appear to want to jump into the river after them. They also seemed unwilling to fire into the cadets.

Niner Squad had no such qualms, and rifles crackled and popped on the shore.

The Puma slid across the sky and disappeared over the trees. Bolan slogged up the riverbank. He got Franco on his feet and retrieved his weapons. "Get under the trees!"

Niner Squad retreated beneath the forest canopy. Franco tugged at Bolan's arm, and he looked where Franco was pointing. The hunter seemed to have recovered from his panic the moment he was out of the river. In the failing light Bolan saw a log. He blinked and he saw a crocodile pretending to be a log as hard as it could. The soldier had never seen a crocodile having a panic attack before, but they were territorial animals, and this one had just had about two tons of helicopter fall out of the sky into its domain. The crocodile sat in the reeds along the shore with its legs stretched out to either side, its mouth partially open and its eyes slammed shut and hyperventilating as it waited for the rest of the sky to fall.

"Déjeuner!" Franco proclaimed.

It was a French word Bolan knew—breakfast!

"Hammer!"

"Yes, Sergeant!"

"Get off the shore and find us a campsite! Get a fire going!"

"On it, Sergeant!"

Bolan nodded at Franco, who raised his revolver from the thong around his neck and took careful aim between the croc's eyes. The pistol made a single small "pop" and put an end to the creature's moral devastation.

IT WASN'T pangolin kebab, much less fricasseed rope squirrel, but Franco's crocodile on a stick wasn't bad. As a general rule, the only reason Bolan would eat a reptile was because he was hungry. They did not taste like chicken. Franco had sliced the crocodile's tail filets bacon thin, rubbed them with salt and spices from one of his beeswax-lined leather pouches and threaded them over sharpened sticks. The last of the hoarded coffee, tea and cocoa packets from the plane and French ration packs got heated up in the aluminum canteens and passed around. Hammer spoke the squad's mind. "Sarge?"

"Yeah?"

"Tomorrow is it, isn't it?"

Niner Squad grew very quiet around the campfire. For a moment there was no sound except for the crocodile stick meat sizzling over the fire.

"They won't come for us in the night, and given the thickness of the bush around here they have a few deployment problems. They'll have marked the spot where we crashed and returned to the village. We can expect them to be back tomorrow around dawn. They'll find the closest open spot to the crash they can land in and deploy Caesar and an oversize squad of his men. The chopper will act as a spotter as Caesar runs us down. Nenad and a few of the Iranians will form a smaller fire team and stay on the chopper. If they spot us from the air, they'll most likely leapfrog ahead and try to find a spot to deploy ahead and cut us off. They'll probably fight a delaying action to give Caesar time to catch up. That's when the trap swings shut."

Niner Squad considered this bit of news.

"What about your friend Freedom Train?" Shelby suggested.

"He'll either get here in time or he won't."

That irrefutable fact was met with another sober silence. Eischen cleared his throat. "Sarge?"

"Yeah?"

"What if he doesn't?"

"Then we kill them, Ace. We kill them all."

Eischen gulped.

Johnson put on his game face. “So what’s our strategy, Sarge?”

“A lot of tomorrow we’re going to have to play by ear. Ideally we need to find a clearing where our ride can land. Worse comes to worst he can winch us up two at a time through the canopy, but we don’t want to try to do that in the middle of a firefight on the ground much less with an armed enemy helicopter in the air. The easiest way would be to follow the river until it widens, but Nenad will be expecting that. So we’re going to head straight into the bush. We leave in an hour.”

Niner Squad glanced around at one another in new alarm.

“Another night march, Sarge?” Metard asked. Even by the kindness of firelight the maimed young man looked wan and exhausted.

“We have two flashlights from the plane and my tactical. I’ve been hoarding the batteries. Now we use them. We finish eating. Rest for an hour, and then we start walking. Not a forced march but a walk. We are going to walk all night. I don’t want to start tomorrow with them hot on our heels. I want Nenad, Caesar and the Iranians to be shocked that we are nowhere in sight come morning. I want some breathing room to have choices. At dawn we’ll rest for a while and start walking again. If we come upon an ideal ambush point, we might just take up residence. Caesar will not run us down. If extraction doesn’t come, then it’s going to be a fight, and that fight will be at a time and a place of our choosing.”

“Goddamn right!” Hudjak snarled.

Bolan rose to his feet. “Our enemies outnumber us, but we are the superior force. Quds Force are terrorists, not soldiers. They are the kind of people who get other people to strap bombs on themselves and commit their atrocities for them. Here in the jungle they are going to have to do their own fighting. They are not ready for what Niner Squad has become.”

“Fuckin’ ay!” Metard declared.

“Nenad is a soldier, but his men are gangsters—river gangsters. Not jungle fighters. They are not ready for what Niner Squad has become."

Jovich rose and the rest of the squad stood up with him. "No way in hell they're ready for us."

"Caesar's men are jungle fighters, but they come from a spray-and-pray firefight philosophy. They have been terrorizing unarmed villages for far too long. They are not ready for what you have become."

Eischen intoned Bolan's words from the battle in the glade. "We shoot them until they're all down or we are."

Bolan shoved his right hand out into the middle of the circle. The rest of the squad huddled up and put their hands on top of his. "And though we walk through the valley of the shadow of death, we shall fear no evil. For we are Niner Squad, the apex predators and the meanest sons of bitches in the valley."

"Amen, Sergeant," Johnson said.

"Amen."

"On me, call out!" Bolan looked around and saw the steel in the backbone of his people. "Niner!"

The squad instantly shouted back. "Squad!"

"Niner!"

"Squad!"

"Niner!"

"Squad!"

Bolan raised his hand beneath the squad's, and they snapped their hands down to break the huddle. "I'm going to go make a phone call. Be ready to move in an hour."

"FREEDOM TRAIN AIRLINES," Grimaldi answered. "How can I be of assistance?"

Bolan glanced up into the night sky through a break in the canopy. "Where are you?"

"I'm in the CAR, still in the capital."

Bolan's heart sank. A rough guesstimate of their position relative to Bangui, CAR, told him Grimaldi and Dragonslayer were at least six hundred miles away. "What's her status?"

"I got our girl through customs and got her fueled and armed. She is currently stripped for speed and passenger transport."

Dragonslayer was a fascinating aircraft. She had started as a civilian helicopter with extensive modifications. The mods had come on in such a steady stream that there was hardly anything left of the original aircraft. She had become distinctly modular. Dragonslayer's two main jobs, and they often coincided, were to pass herself off as a civilian aircraft and then transform into a troop transport for Farm personnel or a gunship to back them up. Niner Squad would be packed like sardines in her cabin but unlike the Alouette Bolan had mutilated and destroyed, Dragonslayer had two engines and they were behemoths. They were like a pair of 1955 Chevys on a 1935 frame. It was quite possible that Dragonslayer had the highest power-to-weight ratio of any helicopter on the planet. She was a black program one-off. She did not have to pass any government regulations or standardizations. Her only responsibility was to meet Grimaldi's ever-evolving, semierotic, aeronautical fever dreams.

"How soon can you be airborne?"

Grimaldi made an unhappy noise. "I'm having some problems with the locals."

"What kind of problems?"

"Problems that my high-school French and a tidy sum of money are still having problems with. I could almost swear someone is working against us."

"Have you spoken to the French consulate?"

"I have. Henri really likes my gold Krugerrands, however I'm starting to get the feeling he really likes gold dinars, as well. I'm beginning to think this is turning into a bidding war."

"Bid higher. Tell me the exact situation."

"Our girl is in a hangar on the airfield. She is fueled, stub wings are up, external fuel tanks fueled and loaded and I got a .30-caliber gun pod."

"And?"

"And I got some disreputable types standing around outside the hangar with rifles waiting for the bidding war to end."

"How many?"

"Six."

"Just so you know, the bad guys have an Aérospatiale Puma."

"I can run rings around a Puma," Grimaldi scoffed.

"They have a 20 mm cannon in the starboard door."

"Oh." Grimaldi lost a bit of his superior tone. "Remember that thing I said about getting through customs and stripped for speed?"

"I do."

"Our girl isn't wearing any armor."

"Then there's a real chance you're going to have a dogfight on your hands, buddy."

"I live to serve!"

"The enemy is going to make contact with us tomorrow, and I can't avoid it. I need you in the air, ASAP."

"All right, I'm not going to wait on the officials. I'm busting the girl out of there."

"You said there are six of them."

"Yeah, but I have an idea."

"What's that?" Bolan asked.

"It's Friday night."

"And?"

"I'm going to go see how many of the French Foreign Legionnaires are out on the town on their weekend pass, how many of them have American accents and how many of them would like to earn some cash beating up some local goons."

"Well, you are a people person."

"I am that," Grimaldi replied.

"Call me when you're close."

Grimaldi's voice grew deadly serious. "I will be there, Sarge. I goddamn guaran-goddamn-tee it."

It was a good morning for a walk. The sky above was a cloudless blazing blue when you could see it through the trees. The morning fog had lifted, and beneath the canopy it was still nice and cool. Niner Squad moved at a sedate pace. Breakfast had been an all-the-cold-crocodile-you-could-eat buffet followed by a nap. Niner Squad had gorged itself and slept like a log. Sleeping and eating boded well for their confidence and attitude. Bolan took his small tube of gun grease and had the squad check its weapons from the dunking in the river and then lube the actions. Most of the squad had emptied a magazine at the enemy helicopter the day before. They were down to five mags each. They weren't force-marching or cutting trail with their *pangas*. Franco led them from one game path to the next, lazily zigzagging in a vaguely northerly direction. They were going to be rescued or there was going to be a fight.

There was no hurry.

Rudipu called back from his position on point with Franco. "Sarge!"

Bolan trotted forward. Franco and Rudipu had found a break in the canopy. The soldier motioned the squad forward. The morning sun slanted down in golden rays on green grass. Butterflies flitted in the sunlight and landed on the brilliantly colored bell-shaped flowers that exploded with the access to light.

Shelby sighed. "Little slice of heaven."

"Goddamn Garden of Eden," Hudjak agreed.

Eischen had more things on his mind than pastoral beauty. "You think the Freedom Train can make a landing here?"

The problem was that it was a little slice of heaven. More of a cathedral than a glade. "It'll be tight."

"You aren't thinking extraction site, Sarge." Johnson glanced around the area. "You're thinking killing ground."

"It had occurred to me, Hammer."

Everyone looked up as rotors thumped in the distance.

Jovich looked at Bolan hopefully. "Is that—?"

"He would have called, Jock-itch."

"You think the Iranians will deploy their fire team here, Sarge?" Johnson asked.

Bolan shot his squad leader a grin. "God I hope so." Grins spread around the squad. The Executioner nodded. "By the numbers. Just like last time. Break into pairs. I want the glade in a cross fire. Remember, they have a cannon. We're going to let them deploy their team and let the helicopter move back into search mode before we fire. Wait for my signal."

"Niner Squad, by teams!" Johnson called. "Move out!"

Niner Squad took position in twos. Shelby and Eischen were closest to Bolan and Rudipu. The helicopter roared overhead and orbited the glade. It was the same blue Puma from the previous afternoon. Despite the rotor noise, Rudipu spoke quietly. "You think they know we're here, Sarge?"

Bolan watched the helicopter circle. "They suspect it."

The helicopter slid out of sight and the sound of its rotors moved off. Shelby muttered, "Well, just, fuckies..."

The helicopter roared back, booming inches over the canopy. A grenade clattered down through the canopy and fell with a dull thud in the loam in front of Snake. "Grenade!" Eischen shouted. The cadet threw himself on top of it without hesitation. Bolan charged forward. He grabbed Shelby and slung her behind a tree. Niner Squad hugged dirt for long seconds. No whip-crack of a frag or thud of HE detonation occurred. Bolan peered around the tree.

Eischen lay facedown and unmoving.

Rotors thundered overhead and more grenades clattered

down. "Into the glade! Go! Go! Go!" Bolan ordered. Niner Squad charged into the glade, pointing their weapons skyward. The soldier took a deep breath and lunged for Eischen. He grabbed him by his pack straps and hauled him up. Beneath him a cylindrical, Russian military dark green grenade was hissing away. Whatever was coming out of it was colorless.

Eischen's lips and cheeks were turning blue. Bolan's lungs burned as he flung Eischen into a fireman's carry and ran for the glade. "Hammer! Weapons on full-auto! When he comes back around give him a mag each! Donger! Medical kit!"

"You heard the man!" Johnson shouted. "Set your selectors to rock and roll and follow me!"

Bolan ran into the sunshine and placed Eischen on the ground.

King ran up and butterflied his pack open. He looked at his friend's blue face anxiously. "Jesus, Sarge, what'd they hit him with? Nerve gas?"

"No, if they had he'd be doing the herky-jerkys and so would I. He's out cold." Bolan rummaged through their supplies. "If I had to bet it's Kolokol-1."

"Sarge?"

"The layman's term would be *knockout gas.* It's a Russian incapacitating agent. It usually takes effect in one to three seconds after breathing and knocks you out for two to six hours. It—"

The helicopter appeared high in the sky over the little glade. Bolan had no time for it as he found the EpiPen. All around him AKs sprayed brass as Niner Squad opened on full-auto. Bolan heard the helicopter bank away. The bad guys had already done their damage and marked Niner Squad's position.

"Sarge!" King's voice rose in alarm. "Ace isn't breathing!"

"I know, he didn't just get a whiff of gas." Bolan tore open the EpiPen package. "He threw himself on the grenade and laid in it. In large enough doses the agent suspends the respiratory muscles."

"Jesus! Shouldn't we initiate CPR?"

"The gas shut him down. He has a very powerful depressant drug in his system. There's no guarantee that regular resuscitation would do any good." Bolan stuck two fingers against Eischen's carotid. He had a pulse, but it was weak and thready and Bolan could literally feel it dying away beneath his fingertips. "Even if it did, we don't have time to let him have a six-hour nap. We need to restart him, ASAP."

King looked at the auto-injector as Bolan snapped off the cap. "I thought that was for anaphylactic shock."

"It is, but it's still zero point five milligrams of pure adrenaline."

The eyes of the young Army doctor in the making went wide.

King was right. Epinephrine was for severe allergic reactions and intended to be injected into a large muscle group like the thigh. Injecting it directly into the bloodstream was extremely dangerous. On the other hand, Eischen was going to be brain damaged or dead in another sixty seconds. Bolan stabbed the needle into the red marks his fingers had made against Eischen's left carotid and injected.

The cadet's entire body locked like tetanus. His chest expanded like a balloon in violent inhalation and he sat up like a puppet whose strings had been brutally jerked. "Motherfucker!"

Eischen collapsed back again, jerking, shuddering and eye rolling but conscious and breathing. Bolan heard the helicopter rumble back over, and a loudspeaker blared. "Put down your weapons and surrender! You will not be harmed!"

The squad waited for the chopper's next run, but it never happened. The rotor noise receded into the distance.

Bolan stared down at his chemically conflicted cadet. "Ace, can you walk?"

"I...I...I..." Eischen babbled. "I..."

"Donger, get Ace up and get him walking."

"Right, Sarge!"

Johnson ran up. "Franco found another trail, Sarge. He says there's a river nearby."

Bolan regarded his squad leader dryly. "Didn't know you spoke French, Hammer."

"Well, I don't, Sergeant. I'm taking Spanish at my academy, but Franco talks, and he makes hand gestures, and..." Johnson shrugged. "I get it."

"That's a useful skill, Hammer."

"What's the plan, Sarge?"

"Hammer, they dropped a spread of gas grenades to try to knock some of us out and slow us. The rotors blasted the clearing clean, but as of now this glade is radioactive. They know we're here and we can't defend it. Tell everyone to hold their breath as long as they can as they leave the glade and head straight down Franco's path. Do not expose yourself on the river. Keep an ear out for rotor noise. Now that they know where we are, they will try to deploy a team ahead of us."

King got Eischen to his feet and gave him a shoulder to lean on. The gassed cadet was babbling like a crackhead in midtweak, but he wobbled out of the glade with King's guidance. Rudipu put a fresh magazine into his rifle and racked the action. "You want me on point or hanging back on our six, Sarge?"

"You can stick with me for a few minutes."

"You think they might wait for us to clear out and then come back and drop in their team wearing gas masks?"

"You have a devious mind, Rude."

"Thank you, Sergeant."

"Keep an eye on the sky. I'm going to make a call."

"I was hoping you were going to say that, Sarge!"

Bolan made the call. Grimaldi answered instantly. "Freedom Train Airlines, how may I direct your call?"

Bolan was pleased to hear the sound of rotors and vibration on the other end of the line. "Freedom Train, this is Striker."

"Sarge, you said to call when I was close."

"We are close to reaching the end of this, one way or the other. The enemy has made contact. I need to start making some decisions. Give me your sitrep."

"My plan was magical. I found a dozen likely lads in the

Bangui red-light district. They drove up drunk in a truck, jumped out waving papers and shouting in French and English. Gotta love those legionnaires. Being Americans, they were very sympathetic to our cause. Well, actually, only two of them were Americans. Two were Canadians, two were from Djibouti and the rest were Russians, but I'll tell you, Sarge, a finer bunch of fellows you never met. I explained the situation to them. Kids always draw sympathy. And a healthy chunk of change always draws genuine empathy. Anyway, they hopped out of the truck, waved some blank requisition forms like they meant something and then jumped those poor guards and pounded them like nails. I paid them off and took off. They drove back to their barracks with big grins and another story to tell." Grimaldi sighed in mock sadness. "Oh, and I'll have you know, by the way, that it will take me some time to rebuild my reservoir of goodwill with the powers that be in the Central African Republic."

"Where are you?"

"I crossed the Ubangi River an hour ago. I am over the DRC and en route to your position."

"How soon?"

"No bullshit assessment?"

"Please."

"The fact remains the boys at M'Poko International are very well aware I made a hostile takeoff. They have contacted the DRC. There is chatter. It's all in French, but they are not happy campers. If I had to bet the DRC is scrambling whatever they have to scramble, which last I heard was a few eighties vintage MiGs, Mikoyans and Sukhois in various states of repair. Regardless, that means I am flying under the radar. I'm talking nap of the jungle. It's going to be a few hours before I get there."

"Copy that, Freedom Train. Be advised the Puma is in the area. They have our general location. I cannot guarantee a decent landing zone. You may have to deploy a canopy penetrator and hoist us out by twos."

Grimaldi's voice went sly. "Don't worry about that."

Bolan allowed himself a tiny glimmer of hope. "What have you got?"

"Well, I got bored while I was waiting so I went on the internet."

"And?"

"Well, fascinating stuff. During the British Malayan campaign from 1948 to 1960, the Brits really started using helicopters in earnest."

"Yes…"

"Well, the Malayan jungle is thick."

"I know," Bolan said. "I've been there."

"Well, I know you know, but the Brits pioneered dropping large amounts of dynamite to clear a space a chopper could land in. Blowing holes in the rain forest is kind of non-PC these days, but…"

"You have dynamite?"

"Where there's a will there's a way." Bolan could sense Grimaldi grinning. "I got a shit load of it. I'm telling you, if this bird takes one bullet in the wrong place I will eclipse the sun. You need to be well out of the way when I go Armageddon, Sarge, but I can blast us a landing field."

"You rule, Jack."

"Yeah, well, you know…"

"Call me when you're close," Bolan instructed.

"Stay safe."

"Striker out."

Rudipu bounced up and down on the balls of his feet happily. "The Freedom Train is coming?"

"It's on its way, but it may be a few hours."

The cadet nodded. "That's okay."

"Is it?"

"Sarge—" Rudipu casually placed his rifle across his shoulders "—we can take these guys."

"Rude, do you know what hubris is?"

Rudipu peered into his eyebrows for long moments. "Vanity that offends the gods, Sarge?"

"That's correct, Rude."

"I like to think of it as confidence in the skills the sergeant has instilled in myself and my squad. Besides, Sarge." Rudipu grinned up at Bolan. "You are the angry god of my universe, and my faith is strong."

Bolan peered down at the cadet.

Rudipu cleared his throat. "Right! Company suck up! Nobody likes him!"

The Executioner nodded. "We're walking, Rude."

"Right, Sarge!"

Bolan and Rudipu took up a loose rearguard position and followed Niner Squad north.

“There!” The raccoon-eyed skull of Nenad’s face split into a horrible smile as he pointed. “We deploy there! Perfect!” It wasn’t exactly perfect, but the break in the canopy would allow them to rappel, and that meant Nenad, Sami, as well as Rhage, Pakzad and the two Quds Force enforcers with them could deploy a klick and a half just west of the commando and his underage charges. He opened the breech on his rifle’s grenade launcher and slid in a Romanian HE shell. He had tried to be nice. He had tried to send the little children to sleep with the gas grenades. But it seemed there would have to be a real fight. Nenad slid the breech shut with a clack. The blast grenade had a plastic casing to avoid fragmentation damage to either friend or foe. Ideally they wanted the children alive, and bouncing them around was better than tearing them to shreds. Even brain-damaged or with concussions the children could still be put to a myriad of purposes, and in the sad event some of the children were killed? Nenad smiled to himself.

No one liked picking shrapnel out of their food.

The chopper dropped to tree level and Nenad tossed his rope out the side. The door gunner swept the jungle below with his sight, but nothing moved except for the treetops whipping in the rotor wash. “Clear!”

“We go!” Nenad kicked out into space and slid down the rope like a spider. Pakzad went out the other side. Nenad’s boots hit mud and he held the rope for Sami. In moments the six-man fire team was on the ground and the helicopter pulled away, trailing the ropes behind it.

Rhage and Pakzad looked determined. The two Quds Force soldiers clutched their sterile submachine guns and looked about the jungle warily as the sound of the chopper faded into the distance. Nenad shook his head. City boys. They missed their air-conditioned office in Arua already. He hoped they could shoot straight. Nenad found himself invigorated to be out in the field again. He had been spending too much time in his office, as well. "Sami?"

Sami had been born deep in the woods before heading downriver to seek his fortune in the city. He instantly found the game trail that led to the pool, and it conveniently headed south. Sami drew his *panga.* "This way."

Captain Rhage glanced around the little open area. A small part of him really didn't feel like leaving it. A huge part of him did not like ceding authority to Nenad, but Rhage knew he was literally lost in the woods at the moment. "How shall we proceed? A skirmish line?"

"Sami has been in the woods before. We will let him go a little bit ahead and—"

Sami staggered backward like he'd been sucker punched in the jaw as the rifle shot cracked out. He fell flat in the mud with the top of his head missing. Nenad dropped and he heard the sonic crack of the next rifle shot passing over his head. His combat-trained ear told him the shots came from two different rifles. An invisible hammer struck Rhage in the chest, and blood exploded out of his back. He sat down hard, and his two troopers began firing wildly into the woods.

A third rifle shot cracked and one of the Quds Force troopers fell spinning into a puddle. Nenad's tactical mind made a heartbeat-quick calculation. Two-man sniper team. They had gone for the tracker and then the commanders of the fire team in a descending order of target priorities. The third shot was foolish. It gave Nenad a vague triangulation. The Serb popped up. He pushed the trigger button on his grenade launcher and his weapon belched pale yellow fire.

BOLAN FLEW BACKWARD on the wings of a superheated pressure wave. Heat and smoke filled his lungs, but when he hit the dirt hardwired instincts made him slap out and do a back roll. Lights pulsed between his eyes, and his ears rang like bells as he came up on one knee and his BXP filled his hand.

"Sarge!" he could dimly hear Rudipu screaming, "Sarge! Sarge!"

Bolan rose to his feet and woozily dropped to one knee again. He yawned to try to clear the ringing in his ears, and the action elicited a violent coughing jag. The coughing made his heart make a fist. His right eye hurt and his face felt wet. Bolan brought his hand to his face and it came away covered with blood. The blast had slammed his scope into his face and gouged his cheek open.

"Sarge!"

Bolan heard his own voice from far away. "I said one shot each and then fall back to the next position, Rude."

"Sorry, Sarge. I missed Nenad and got excited."

Bolan grabbed Rudipu's shoulder and hauled himself back up. "My rifle."

Rudipu grabbed Bolan's rifle and looked at it in dismay. "Sarge?"

Bolan examined the old Enfield Enforcer. The forward lens was shattered, and the scope tube was clearly out of alignment. Bolan's blood smeared the grip and the bolt. "Looks pretty bad, doesn't it?"

Rudipu gave Bolan a very leery look. "Sarge, you look pretty bad."

The forward lens and the cross hairs were somehow intact. Bolan winced as he squeezed his right cheek muscle. Blood dripped down and smeared over the reticule.

"Eew! Sarge, are you—" Rudipu's jaw dropped in awe. "Sarge, you are totally sick, and I mean that in the good way."

Bolan walked back to where he'd been blasted by the grenade and dropped the rifle in the flattened underbrush. He took off his bandolier of .308 ammo and gave it a few smears of blood for good measure before dropping it in the grass.

Rudipu glanced back toward the little clearing. "You think they're coming?"

"No. Nenad just lost three men, including his tracker. He doesn't know where the rest of Niner Squad is. He's going to sit tight and wait for Caesar to come up."

"So what are we going to do?"

Bolan unscrewed his suppressor tube and spun on the grenade-launching muzzle attachment. He took out his last rifle grenade and clicked it onto the muzzle. "We're going to fade back and wait for Caesar to come up."

The soldier's sat phone vibrated. Rudipu's face was heartbreakingly eager as Bolan answered. "Striker."

"Sarge, this is Freedom Train. I have your position on GPS. ETA ten minutes."

KAYIZI'S VOICE WAS barely a whisper above the sounds of the jungle. "Brother Obua!"

Obua crawled on his belly like a snake and made even less noise. They had heard the gun battle and approached with extreme caution. Obua lay beside Kayizi, who pointed. Obua's eyes narrowed. The trunk of a huge old ironwood tree had been blackened by some kind of blast and the grass around it flattened. Off to one side lay a rifle and a bandolier of ammo. The two men nodded at each other and began a torturously slow crawl around the rifle's little perimeter looking for trip wires or mines. After a complete circuit, Obua made a nerve-racking crawl to within arm's reach of the rifle and pulled it in. He took a look at the bloody and damaged weapon, and a smile crossed his face. Obua made a call. "Nenad, is Brother Obua."

"Where are you?"

"I am at the commando's last-known position. Tell me, did you fire a grenade at him?"

"I didn't have line of sight, but I lobbed one in his general direction."

"Pakzad is with you?"

"Yes, why?"

"Send him," Obua said.

Nenad switched from English to Ngala. "Are you using him for a decoy?"

"My purpose is twofold, but yes."

"Very well."

Pakzad blundered out of the underbrush. Kayizi shot Obua a look to say that hippos made less noise. Obua relaxed slightly as no bullet took off the Iranian's head. Obua hissed. Pakzad snapped his weapon around. Obua rolled his eyes and muttered low. "Hey! You! Iran boy!"

Pakzad located the sound and walked over. All pretense at stealth had been lost. However, Pakzad was blissfully free of bullet holes. The Iranian dropped to a knee beside them. "What is— *Bismillah!*"

Obua grinned over Kayizi's find. "This is the commando's long rifle?"

"He is inhumanly accurate with it." Pakzad took the weapon, and his eyes widened as he examined it. His mind instantly saw the American staring down the scope of his rifle, and he could almost feel the sudden, unexpected blast of the high-explosive grenade. He felt no empathy whatsoever as he imagined the rifle scope's eyepiece violating one of the cold blue eyes that had intimidated him so. He felt a very ugly sense of satisfaction. It was an eye that would never draw bead on himself, his men or anyone else ever again. "He's hurt. He is hurt very badly, and probably not just his eye."

Kayizi had moved at a crouch a little way from the blast. He looked at footprints. "The little cadet and the commando."

"They formed a sniper pair," Pakzad acknowledged.

Kayizi nodded at the dragging boot prints of the commando. "He leans heavily on the little one." Kayizi grinned broadly at a gouge in the soft soil that repeated every five feet. "He uses the little one's rifle as a crutch."

Obua took out his phone. "Caesar."

"Brother Obua."

"Caesar, I..." He looked up at the sound of rotors. "Choppers." Obua scanned the treetops. "Two of them."

"I have ears, brother. Sky belongs to heaven. We do God's work on his good green earth."

"His will be done, Caesar. The American is wounded, wounded most sorely."

"Link up with Nenad."

"Yes, Caesar." Obua rose, joined by Pakzad. Kayizi walked back.

Segawa's voice grew prophetic over the phone. "I am but minutes behind you, brother. We shall—"

Suddenly a rifle grenade thumped from somewhere out in the bush.

"Caesar!" Obua screamed.

Obua's scream cut short as eighty grams of RDX sent coiled steel wire expanding outward in a lethal sphere with the three men at its epicenter.

GRIMALDI FLEW FOR HIS life. Bolan had made a mistake. The enemy chopper was not a Puma, it was a Super Puma. An easy mistake to make. The Puma and the Super Puma had nearly the same lines, only the Super Puma, was super-size. She was bigger, stronger and faster than the first born of the lineage. Dragonslayer was much faster and far more nimble, but helicopter dogfights were nothing like fights between airplanes. A helicopter could do interesting things, such as fly nap of the earth and spin 360 degrees on its axis. To add to the fun, the Super Puma had a 20 mm cannon in a door mounting, which meant he could traverse his fire in an arc. He could not, however, point his weapon directly forward or backward in line with his chopper, and he could only fire from one side of the aircraft.

Grimaldi had a single .30-caliber machine gun under one of his stub wings, and it could only fire directly forward like the guns of a jet fighter. He had flown to northeast DRC on external fuel tanks and had ejected. On his stub wing opposite his gun pod he had an external helicopter cargo pod with five hundred sticks of dynamite in it. A stick of dynamite contained roughly 2.1 megajoules of energy. As Grimaldi understood it, an MJ was approximately the equivalent of a one-ton vehicle moving at one hundred miles per hour. Multiplied by five hundred, Grimaldi had a nice, round 1,250 megajoules of energy to play with.

He thought it might just make a nice sunroof in the jungle canopy.

On the other hand, his opponent was firing 20 mm HE incendiary shells at him, and it wouldn't take much of a near miss to turn Grimaldi and Dragonslayer into a spectacular midair special effect. The Super Puma's 20 mm cannon also outranged Grimaldi's .30 by about a factor of three. It was making for an interesting dogfight. The Stony Man pilot had two missions. He had to blow a clearing out of the jungle, and then he had to extract Niner Squad. The enemy had only one job, and that was to stop him from doing one or both.

Grimaldi streaked out of cannon range to set himself up for another maneuver. His opponent let him. He flicked a glance at his GPS tracker. Niner Squad was very close. In fact at the moment the Super Puma was closer to them than he was. That told him that they had a very good idea where Niner Squad was. That told him Niner Squad was engaged on the ground. The enemy pilot was perfectly content to let Grimaldi waste time and fuel.

Grimaldi flicked a glance at his fuel gauge and his clock. He was starting to run into a fuel debt situation. The clock also told him that if the DRC air force had scrambled their MiGs, he was running into a time debt situation, as well. Grimaldi needed to make an LZ and get rid of the Super Puma once and for all.

He decided to kill two birds with one stone.

The ace pilot tapped the console on his armrest. "Sarge, I'm going to blow a hole!"

Bolan's voice sounded disturbingly strained to Grimaldi's ear. "Now or not at all, Jack."

Grimaldi tapped off. He yanked his stick back, shoved his throttle forward and climbed into the sun. Dragonslayer's twin engines roared and her composite rotor blades slammed the sky for altitude. He took his pride and joy up to ten thousand feet and took a moment to enjoy the view. The Super Puma had no radar and Grimaldi knew he had turned himself into a speck that had disappeared in the glare. He shoved his stick forward and banked around into a hard steep dive straight out of the sun. With the latest engine and body mods, Grimaldi's personal estimate for Dragonslayer's never exceed speed was 250 miles per hour. The speed gauge was crawling up into the 270s and Dragonslayer was taking on an almost harmonic vibration.

Grimaldi watched the jungle of the Congo rush up at him. The Super Puma's pilot suddenly realized what was happening and started evasive maneuvers. Grimaldi thumbed his gun trigger. He was diving nearly straight down, and gravity had become his machine gun's ally rather than its nemesis. He had plunging fire and only friction to slow his bullets. Grimaldi smiled as the Super Puma dived for the deck and began a tight, twisting circle yards above the canopy. It was a good tactic. In a dive this steep and this fast, Grimaldi could not maneuver his gun effectively. The Super Puma pilot was going to let him make his gun run, spin on his axis and put a burst of 20 mm HEI right up Grimaldi's tail. He dived straight at the center point of the Super Puma's evasive orbital circumference like a kamikaze pilot diving at an aircraft carrier.

Like a dive bomber, Grimaldi punched the button on his stub wing controls and the explosive bolts fired and released the cargo pod.

Dragonslayer moaned as its pilot yanked back on his stick and pulled out of his dive.

The teardrop-shaped cargo pod fell past the Super Puma scant yards from its rotors and punched through the jungle canopy. Five hundred sticks of dynamite did a mighty impressive job of imitating a micromushroom cloud.

The Super Puma disappeared inside of it.

Grimaldi banked around and grinned. He had made himself a little microversion of the Tunguska Event in Russia. He had a beautiful, smoking little circle of knocked-over trees surrounding a mighty tidy little crater. He couldn't exactly land on it, but he could hover scant feet above it. Slightly south there was a second burning hole in the canopy that looked suspiciously like a crashed helicopter event. Grimaldi tapped his communications icon. "Niner Squad! LZ established! Go! Go! Go!"

Leaves rained down as the world ended a few klicks east. Bolan leaned on Rudipu as they rejoined Niner Squad, and he wasn't faking it for the benefit of those tracking him. Johnson ran forward. "Sarge! What happened?"

Rudipu hunched his shoulders in shame. "I got trigger happy. The bad guys got a fix and lobbed a grenade at us."

"Damn it, Rude! What did the sarge say about fire discipline?" Hudjak came over and threw Bolan's arm over his shoulder. The blond giant eased Bolan onto a fallen log. Von Kwakkenbos was instantly at his side. King squatted in front of Bolan like a baseball catcher and peered deeply into his eyes.

Hudjak rounded on Rudipu. "Tell me you got at least one of them."

"I got two!" Rudipu protested. "Sarge took out Pakzad's commanding officer, then he pulled a grenade maneuver of his own. He took out Obua, that tracker dude." Rudipu paused a moment. "And Pakzad."

Niner Squad looked around at one another. For a brief second Pakzad had almost been something like a member of the team.

"We part as friends," Johnson said, misquoting Pakzad. "When next we meet we're enemies."

Rudipu gave the squad a quick debriefing of events.

King frowned deeply into Bolan's face. "Your pupils look fine, Sarge, and if you're kicking ass and taking names I don't think you have a concussion," the aspiring doctor concluded.

"I don't like the cough, though, and you don't want to look in a mirror. I could try to sew up your face, but I think Snake would do a better job."

"Tylenol with codeine," Bolan rasped. "And water with any powdered sports drink that's left."

King cracked open the med bag. Von Kwakkenbos produced a horded packet of glucose, caffeine and phenylamine and shook it up in her water bottle. Bolan needed all of it. The next twenty minutes of his life was most likely going to suck hard. Bolan popped the pills and tilted back most of the contents of the bottle. He wiped his chin and took a long slow breath. He winced as stabbing pain radiated through his chest from just left of center.

Bolan looked up and found himself locking eyes with Franco. The hunter looked like he might start crying again. They both knew it was bad. Metard sat on a rock cradling his stump. His eyes were closed, and he seemed to be concentrating on nothing more than breathing. Eischen was twitching and seemed to be taking great interest in everything and nothing.

Bolan took another experimental deep breath. He winced as it went about as bad as the first one. "Hammer."

Conversation ceased. "Sergeant?"

"Go," Bolan ordered. "Take the squad and get out of here."

Niner Squad was horrified.

"No way, Sarge!" Johnson shook his head vehemently. We're Niner Squad! None left be—"

Bolan surged to his feet. He grabbed Johnson by the front of his pack straps and lifted him onto his toes. "You will get your squad to the LZ, Squad Leader! That is a direct order! You will load the squad and…" Bolan dropped Johnson as his knees nearly buckled beneath him. His lungs weren't burned, but he had breathed in far too much heat and smoke. Medically a blast wave had had its way with him. It was a medical miracle that he didn't have a concussion, but the fact was he had taken more nonspecific blast damage than he could afford. High explosive had rippled through him and shaken him like a terrier with a bedroom slipper. His insides were bruised if not hematomaed. The exhaustion of the past week that he had ruthlessly denied finally fell on him, and his injuries like a sack of hammers. Bolan felt like he could have a heart attack at any second.

His voice dropped into a Clint Eastwood snarl. "Hammer, listen to me. We are out of time. Meat is done. Ace is a vegetable for the next six hours. You have to cover a mile through the jungle, maybe two to reach the LZ. Caesar is on his way and doing it at the run. If we stick and fight, half of the squad will get killed. I'm not going to let that happen. Neither are you. So I'm going to stick around, delay them for a little while, and you're taking the squad home."

Johnson's eyes went huge. "Sarge…"

"Who are you?" Bolan clasped his chest.

The cadet stood tall. "Hammer, Sergeant! Squad leader of Niner Squad!"

"Then take the squad home, Hammer."

Johnson saluted. "Yes, Sergeant."

Bolan saluted back. "Hammer, the man picking you up. His name is Jack, and he's a friend of mine. Tell him…" Bolan broke into a coughing fit. "Tell him…" Bolan covered his mouth with the back of his hand. When he took his hand away the back of his fist was covered with a spray of blood dots.

"Yes, Sergeant." Tears spilled down the young man's face. "I'll tell him."

"Then go."

"Niner Squad! Move out for the LZ!"

Just about every member started to raise an objection. Johnson's voice thundered in a credible imitation of Bolan in sergeant mode. "Sergeant's orders! Move!"

Niner Squad began to move out toward the smoking demolition zone Grimaldi called an LZ. The squad spontaneously stopped. Shelby turned and snapped off a salute and the rest of the squad followed. Bolan saluted back. Well over half the squad looked ready to turn on the waterworks and disobey orders.

Johnson's voice was iron. "The sarge bought us our ticket! Now he's buying us time to make the train! We do not waste a second of it! Move! Move! Move!" Niner Squad cast stricken looks backward, but King grabbed Eischen, Hudjak helped Metard and Niner Squad disappeared by twos and followed their squad leader into the bush. Von Kwakkenbos ran back weeping openly. Johnson didn't roar for order.

Blondie took a knee beside Bolan and sobbed. "Miss you already."

"Miss you, too."

"Call me Roos."

"How about I call you *baby?*"

She crushed her lips against Bolan's. Hers tasted like tears. His tasted like blood. She pressed something into his hand and ran back after the squad. Rudipu took up the rear guard and cast one last forlorn look at his sergeant. "Sarge…"

"Go, Rude. You know your job. No one gets by you."

Terrible determination filled the young marksman's eyes. "Sarge, none shall pass."

Rudipu disappeared into the trees.

Bolan opened his hand. Von Kwakkenbos had pressed a flight-size mini liquor bottle of South African Amarula Cream upon him. He was really starting to wonder where she was hiding things. Bolan cracked the bottle and raised it. "Roos." He allowed himself one slow sip of the self-proclaimed Spirit of Africa. The elephant-fruit spirit looked like Baileys or Kahlua. What it tasted like was the magical chocolate milk of Africa. Elephants were known to gorge themselves late in the season when the fallen fruit was naturally fermenting, and the soldier knew why. It went smooth and creamy down Bolan's throat. He spit it up in another coughing jag. He smiled at the bottle anyway, capped it and put it in his pocket.

This was it.

Bolan rose and began hobbling toward the enemy. He made it back to a clump of rocks he had noted thirty yards back. It was a natural break in the underbrush, and Niner Squad's trail flowed around it and faded into the bush. It was a footrace, and the bad guys were loping. Bolan sat back heavily against the boulders. The codeine and caffeine were beginning to kick in. Vomiting had ruined the flavor of Amarula in his mouth. He was pleased to feel Roos's kiss still tingling on his lips. He took out his remaining Claymore mine and spiked it into the ground at his boot heels. He didn't feel like he could keep any water down, but he poured the rest of his canteen over his face and head and enjoyed the sensation.

He set down the canteen as he heard footfalls and the rhythmic breathing of runners behind him. Bolan put his thumb on the detonator. Niner Squad was going home. None left behind. Franco was going to get a fresh start and a new set of teeth. Von Kwakkenbos would live to fly the friendly skies again.

It hadn't been a bad last mission, and turned out far better than he expected.

He regretted Metard's hand, but between him, Rudipu and Johnson, Metard was the one most likely to end up President—and that was all right.

Bolan had served worse.

He had absolute faith in Grimaldi. All that was left was for Bolan himself to do his part. He took a breath and held it as Segawa's platoon began flowing around both sides of the rock formation. They ran straight ahead like a pack of lions sensing the kill. Bolan counted two, four, five—number six flicked a glance back and the bloody, blast-blackened form he saw lounging behind him in the crotch of the rocks made him widen his eyes in appalled surprise. Bolan hit his detonator.

The Claymore mine exploded. The men on the trail withered as hundreds of ball bearings passed through their bodies. Shouts of horror and alarm broke out behind the rocks. Bolan could sense men skidding to halts in the soft jungle floor. The soldier took out his second to last grenade, pulled the pin and lobbed the bomb up and back behind him. Men screamed as the frag whip-cracked and the shrapnel whipsawed through flesh. Bolan took out his last grenade. It was a smoke. He had brought it to mark his location for extraction, but it would also work to obscure his current position. Bolan levered himself up woodenly and popped smoke. He followed Niner Squad's trail away from the rocks as purple smoke expanded through the trees behind him. Men shouted and screamed in nearly half a dozen languages. Rifles fired and bullets spit through the trees.

"Get him! Get him! Get him!" Segawa shouted.

Bolan shambled through the smoke spitting blood and pushed a detonator pin into his last bit of C-4. He dropped it and chose a tree to lean against. The new, leading element of God's Army charged forward, spraying their rifles like talismans against death. Bolan pressed his detonator remote. It was a small amount of C-4. The three men didn't go sky-high so much as slam dance for a scant second in the orange blast and collapse. Bolan empathized. He'd been in the same situation a short while before. But their work was done.

Bolan still had a job to do. He hadn't put his suppressor back on. He wanted the enemy to focus on him rather than Niner Squad. The soldier stepped out from behind his tree. Two of Segawa's legion barely had time to gawk as Bolan burned them down, before he stepped back behind his tree. He dropped to one knee against his will as something scythed into his left thigh with brutal force. Bolan shoved out his BXP and burned the rest of his magazine into the trees. He reloaded and looked down at where the pain radiated.

A piece of steel was sticking out of his leg.

"Hunga munga," Bolan muttered. It was usually best in combat to leave the wounding agent in. But the metal in his leg was going to slow him. Bolan groaned as he yanked the multibladed weapon free of his flesh and dropped it to the loam. Blood flowed down his leg in a river, and he was acutely aware of its loss. A woman cackled in horrible amusement somewhere nearby. Bolan vainly wished he had another grenade. He limped into the purple smoke instead.

Segawa's voice intoned like a preacher from everywhere and nowhere at once. "You dead, White Leopard! You Uncle Sam's childrens—"

Bolan rammed out his BXP and fired at the sound. He saw

sparks as his bullets ricocheted off of the former rock formation where he'd only recently been. The BXP clacked open on empty. The Executioner reached for another magazine, and there was none left. He reached for his pistol and found Pakzad's with a single magazine in it. He had given his South African RAP pistol to Metard along with his spare magazines. Everything else had gone out the Alouette's door to get airborne. He had thirteen rounds.

Bolan became very aware of the fact that he was punch-drunk on high-explosive shock effect, painkillers and blood loss. He took two steps backward and fell back against a tree trunk. He jerked as a *hunga munga* thunked into the tree trunk inches from his head. He caught a glimpse of black eyes, shark's teeth and dreadlocks. Bolan fired off a pair of double taps and rolled around the trunk. Nine rounds. One of Segawa's men appeared out of the smoke and whirled. Bolan put him down with three in his chest.

Six bullets left.

Another man came screaming through the smoke with a submachine gun in both hands, firing at everything and nothing. "Blood and fire, Caesar! Blood and—"

Bolan gave him two in the face.

Four bullets left.

Segawa howled in victory. "Have you in moments, White Leopard! Have your children in moments next!"

Bolan hit his magazine release. The Browning Hi-Power's mag dropped a half inch out of the magazine well and stopped. Segawa and one of his men popped up and fired. Bullets cracked past Bolan. He fired and the Hi-Power racked open on an empty chamber. Bolan snarled loud enough to be heard. "Shit!"

The soldier coughed, and blood oozed past his lips. He fell to his good knee. Segawa and three of the brethren stepped out of the purple smoke. Bolan let his pistol drop to his side, slide racked open on a smoking empty chamber. Segawa and his men drew their *pangas*. Segawa cocked his head in begrudging admiration. "You had a good run, Commando! But now you die in my fire. Your flesh shall be the bread of—" Bolan's left hand cupped up and slammed his mag back in place. His right thumb hit the Hi-Power's slide release and it slammed home.

Bolan put his front sight on Segawa's chest and pulled the trigger four times.

Julius Caesar Segawa fell down dead in the dirt.

The Executioner dropped his spent, smoking pistol and drew his *panga*.

Mama Waldi came out of the purple smoke with four more of the brethren with her *hunga munga* in hand. Nenad approached from the side. The last Quds Force operative clung to his side like his shadow. She exposed her pointed teeth in a rictus grin and raised her aerial butchering implement. "Eat your flesh, white man. Take your power. Become like what has never been seen."

Nenad drew his bush knife. "First we have some fun with him."

Bolan raised his *panga* between them. "Bring it."

"You bring it." The skull-face grinned at Bolan. "See if you can stand up and bring it to me."

Bolan slowly rose. He coughed, and more blood dribbled from his lips. The soldier laid his machete blade over his shoulder. He figured he had one swing left in him. "You do the rest."

Nenad grinned and shook his head. "Mama, take his good leg off at the knee."

Mama Waldi cocked back her *hunga munga* for the throw. Her remaining men laughed.

Niner Squad's battle cry shook the jungle canopy.

"Niner Squad!"

Niner Squad came out of the trees, bayonets fixed, rifles at shoulder level and firing in rapid semiauto. They were short Eischen, Von Kwakkenbos, Metard and Franco, but the five present cadets charged in a line. Mama Waldi screamed like a banshee and flung her *hunga munga* at Bolan's head. He interposed his *panga*, and the shock ran down his arm as the blades clanged. Shelby's AK went into full-auto, and Mama Waldi staggered back as she took nearly twenty rounds in the chest. Nenad moved to put Bolan between himself and Niner Squad and went for his rifle as the charging squad closed.

Bolan dropped to one knee.

Johnson executed a perfect track-and-field hurdle over the soldier's head. Nenad moaned as the cadet's bayonet went into his belly up to the muzzle. He gasped and folded as Johnson ripped his weapon free. Rudipu ran around Bolan and whipped the butt of his rifle into Nenad's teeth and stood him back up. Hudjak's bayonet thrust to the throat finished him.

Captain Nenad fell dead to the ground. Mama Waldi, the last Quds Force man and Segawa's army lay all around him in a similar state.

Shelby and Jovich moved to the rocks and took up position on the perimeter.

Bolan considered standing back up, then thought better of it. "Where is the rest of your squad, Hammer?"

"Meat and Ace are in the chopper. Blondie and Franco are holding down the LZ."

King secured a field dressing and began binding Bolan's leg.

"Gave you a direct order, Hammer."

"We're Niner Squad, Sergeant." Johnson met his sergeant's gaze without an ounce of regret. "We don't leave anyone behind. I knew it was no use arguing with you, and you were right. If we hadn't gotten our wounded to the LZ, we would have been bogged down and wiped out. But I figured if I brought a fire team back and flanked them we might stand a chance to take them by surprise and extract you."

"Where'd you come up with that brilliant idea?" Bolan inquired.

Johnson tapped a forefinger to his temple knowingly. "I asked myself, what would the sarge do?"

Bolan sighed. A very weary smile crossed his face.

King tied the dressing tight. "We need to get the sarge evacuated stat."

"Right! Rude, switch rifles! Huge, with me!" Johnson took Rudipu's rifle. Hudjak and Johnson each took one of Bolan's arms over their shoulders and the two cadets took the sniper rifle by the barrel and the butt to form a seat for Bolan. They stood up beneath their burden, and Johnson began shouting orders. "Rude, you and Jock-itch! Rear guard! Snake, take point back to the LZ! Niner Squad!" the squad leader commanded. "We're out of here!"

Epilogue

National Naval Medical Center, Bethesda, Maryland.

The nurse leaned her head into Bolan's room. "Mr. Cooper? You have visitors outside."

Bolan lowered the newspaper he was reading. Carmen Delahunt had visited, bringing flowers and stuffed animals among other items on behalf of Stony Man Farm. His room looked like a gift shop. "Send them in."

The nurse gave Bolan an odd smile. "They're waiting outside."

Bolan swung himself around on the bed and grabbed his crutches. It had been a week since they had stabilized him, flown him out Kenya and back to the United States. Bolan could put weight on his leg finally, but he had used up his doctor's allotment of walking and physical therapy for the day—they still weren't letting him have much. What really concerned the doctors was the shock bruising to his internal organs. The only cure for that was rest, and after only a week Bolan was chafing to get out of there. The doctors and nurses had orders from very high up on the food chain that they were authorized to use physical restraints if Bolan tried to push his recovery or escape. The soldier didn't fight it. He ate every ounce of food they gave him, used every second of exercise allowed and in between slept like a log and caught up on current events.

But he had visitors.

Bolan stood, then three-legged it out the door.

"Atten…tion!" Cadet Johnson called.

Niner Squad stood assembled in the hall. Its members wore the full dress uniforms of their respective academies, and the uniforms were immaculate. Their dress shoes were polished mirror bright. The creases of their trousers were sharp enough to shave with. Their dress caps set at exactly the precise line on their heads. Despite the various services their academies represented, the eight cadets' dress uniforms were distinguished by a decidedly nonregulation red-and-gold service patch.

Jack Grimaldi leaned against a door frame in the background and waggled his eyebrows to let Bolan know who had arranged the reunion. He wore a leather flight jacket and it had a suspicious red-and-gold patch on the shoulder, as well.

Bolan nodded at the squad. "At ease."

Niner Squad stood at ease.

"Relax."

Niner Squad relaxed in line. Johnson stepped forward and handed Bolan a pair of photographs. "Blondie and Franco couldn't make it. But we managed to arrange a little something for you."

Bolan looked at the first picture. Franco stood on the prow of his new canoe. He waved happily and grinned into the camera with a mouth full of glinting new gold teeth. The hunter wore a new denim jacket with a red-and-gold patch sewn to the left shoulder, as well. The second photo was an eight-by-ten glossy. Miss Roos von Kwakkenbos wore her full flight-attendant uniform. She posed, smirking coquettishly into the camera over her left shoulder and the patch embroidered on it. She'd written "Love, Blondie XXX OOO" in the lower corner. Bolan smiled. She'd also written her phone number on the back.

Shelby stepped forward and pulled a patch out of her pocket. Her eyes were watering on the verge of tears. "This one's for you, Sarge."

Bolan took the emblem. The shield-shaped patch was a

bloodred field with a gold border, with *9'er* in bold and gold dominating the shield with the word *Squad* beneath it. A pair of stylized lightning bolts bracketed the nine on either side. At the bottom read the Latin words *Nullus Relictus* in block letters—None Left Behind.

Bolan blinked. It had been a very long time since anything besides smoke or war gases had put a sting in his eyes, much less tightened his chest and sent a frog climbing up from some long suppressed part of him into his throat. He ran his thumb over the embroidery. The soldier cleared his throat. "You do good work, Snake."

Tears spilled down Snake's cheeks. "Thank you, Sergeant."

Metard waved his stump. "I'll say she does!"

Laughter broke the misty moment.

Shelby fell back into line. "Niner Squad!" Johnson called. "Attennnn...tion!" Niner Squad snapped ramrod straight. "Salute!"

Eight right hands flew to eyebrow height with parade-ground precision. Bolan set his crutches aside and stood tall. He looked at the line of cadets before him. Bolan saluted the future of the United States Military.

He felt it might be in pretty good hands.

Pizza was definitely going to be on him this night.

* * * * *